Barbara's Blues

She had enough to think about, she reflected, settling into her seat on the north-bound coach: ward notes to copy up as soon as she got back, uniform to press ready for her placement next day, revision she'd promised herself she'd do every night...

Well, that was one thing she could do right now. Barbara reached into her bag, took out a medical textbook and settled down to read.

But all the time, behind the arid words of the text, she heard the insistent beat of music.

Point

NURSES

Barbara's Blues

Bette Paul

■ SCHOLASTIC

Scholastic Children's Books
Commonwealth House, 1–19 New Oxford Street,
London WC1A 1NU, UK
a division of Scholastic Ltd
London ~ New York ~ Toronto ~ Sydney ~ Auckland

First published by Scholastic Ltd, 1996

Copyright © Bette Paul, 1996

ISBN 0 590 13776 X

Typeset by TW Typesetting, Midsomer Norton, Avon

Printed by Cox & Wyman Ltd, Reading, Berks.

All rights reserved

10 9 8 7 6 5 4 3 2 1

The right of Bette Paul to be identified as the author
of this work has been asserted by her in accordance with the
Copyright, Designs and Patents Act, 1988.

Chapter 1

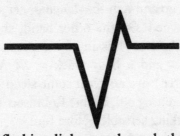

A single flashing light cut through the darkness, picking out flailing limbs, a naked, sweating back, heads rolling, nodding…

Like a bad night in A & E! Barbara Robinson reflected. She grinned across at her brother, crouched over his keyboard. No point in telling him the joke – he'd never hear it! The band was really going now; the noise was almost painful. Barbara could hardly believe that a moment ago she'd been out there in front, singing. Well, the punters seemed to have heard her all right – they'd yelled and cheered as she belted out her final number. And, more important, they'd moved on to the dance floor and the gig was going – at last.

Kenny looked up from the keyboard and caught her eye.

"Cool!" he mouthed, and made a quick thumbs-up sign.

Barbara grinned at him, gave him a single wave and faded off into the darkness. Backstage she could feel the noise banging into the breeze-block walls, as if to bring them down. For a moment she hesitated: she could go and join the dancing, get a taxi later…

She yawned. On the other hand, she had to get the coach back to Brassington in the morning – *this* morning – and a busy week at St Ag's loomed. She'd better leave now, get some sleep, be sensible.

You're getting old, Barbie Robinson, she told herself. Thinking sensible before fun!

Minutes later she was gyrating on the dance floor with the rest of them.

"Barbie! Barbie-gal – you're gonna be late for that bus."

Barbara Robinson pushed her head into the pillow and groaned as Grandma's resonant voice hit her eardrums.

"Come on, Barbie, wake up! I got breakfast on the table."

Sighing, Barbara kicked off the quilt and sat for a moment, holding on to her aching head. Lordy, that music had been so loud in the club last night, and the wine must have come from the dregs of some third-rate agricultural co-op in Central America! She got to her feet and dashed for the bathroom.

"Now, you goin' eat some fry?" Grandma Robinson stood over the kitchen table like a guardsman on duty, frying pan at the ready. "I got sweet potato left from yesterday."

"Ugh – no thank you!" Barbara shuddered. "Lots of coffee and a piece of toast for me. Oh – and I'd love some of your peach preserve," she added, seeing an ominous light in her grandma's eye.

"Well, I don't know," said Gran, parting with the frying pan reluctantly. "Peach toast an' coffee's no start for a busy gal."

"I'm not busy today, Gran," Barbara said. "Sitting on the coach isn't busy, it's restful." And as if to prove it she rested her elbows on the table, supported her chin on her hands and yawned heartily.

Grandma Robinson sniffed. "Well, you surely do need to catch up on some sleep!"

"Yeah – I'll do it on the coach," Barbara agreed. She yawned again and looked around. "Mum out?" she asked, knowing the answer. Her mother was head of the midwifery team at the local hospital and it was her weekend on call.

Grandma Robinson's expression softened. "Call-out," she said. "Might be gone all morning by the sound of it – bet it's a boy."

"Gran, you can't say such things – that's a sexist remark!" Barbara protested.

"No it ain't – that's come right from my own observation. I seen more babies into the world than you've had salt fish dinners, Barbie-gal, and I know as them boys is always slow to leave their home comforts, and—"

"– quick to get back to them," Barbara ended her gran's oft-repeated phrase with a grin.

But her gran nodded seriously. "You can smile, gal, but that's just the truth – I seen it myself many a time."

"I know you have, Gran," Barbara agreed. Back in Jamaica, long before she'd trained in England, Grandma Robinson had acted as unofficial midwife for family and friends. "So, according to you," Barbara went on, "if it's a boy, I won't get to see Mum before I leave?"

"Says she'll call you if she can't get away." Grandma Robinson turned her attention to the toaster. "Coffee's in the pot – how many toasts?"

"Oh, just two, thanks – it's the coffee I need." Barbara reached for the pot.

"You singin' last night?" asked Grandma Robinson, voice edged with disapproval. She thought Barbara should give up all "that singin' nonsense" now she had embarked on her nursing degree.

"Just till midnight," Barbara said defensively – then realized she'd left herself wide open to Grandma's criticism.

"Was three o'clock I heard you come in," she observed.

"Yeah – well, you know what it's like," said Barbara, deliberately vague, "with Kenny on at the Cellar."

Kenny, Barbara's youngest brother, had run his own band since school and was apparently on the brink of success – locally, at least. Everyone in the Robinson family was musical: Kenny had his band, Robbie was a DJ on a local radio station, their mother sang in the gospel choir. Even Grandma played the organ at church, though lately she'd been threatening to retire.

Barbara was no mean performer either. Whether belting out an agonizing blues or breathing a smoochy love song into the mike, she was the most talented of the lot. But there was no danger of her going into show-business like her brothers, she told herself – she wanted security, a regular income – and the status of a respected profession.

"Nursing's a graduate training now," her mother had told her, when Barbara left her accountancy job in the City. "You go get your degree – no knowing where you'll end up."

So, at twenty-two, Barbara Robinson became an undergraduate of the North-West College of Nursing at St Ag's Hospital up in Brassington.

"Why you want to go all that way?" grumbled her gran. "Hospitals in London a-plenty."

"Let her be," said her mother, Serena. "Do her good to get away." Away from what she didn't specify, but Barbara knew she meant away from her brothers and their various musical activities which, sure as eggs, would distract Barbara from her studies.

Because she still loved performing. She loved dressing up in a slinky dress, painting her wide mouth shiny deep purple, slipping her feet into three-inch stilettoes and strolling nonchalantly into the spotlight in some smoky, murky club to hold an audience in the palm of her hand. And getting paid for it too, albeit a mere fraction of what she could have earned if she went professional, as Kenny never failed to point out. And on a morning like this – after the hectic and successful night before – she was certainly tempted: after all, if she didn't have to get the lunch-time coach back to Brassington she'd still be asleep in bed with a fair-sized cheque tucked under her pillow.

"Ought to give all that stuff up now you're training." Grandma's voice broke into her thoughts.

"Give what up, Gran?" Barbara dropped a blob of deep yellow jam on to her toast and watched it meld in with the butter before she picked it up and bit at it. "Mmmmmm – this is good!"

Grandma ignored the flattery. "Give up stayin' out late, singin' in clubs. Who's ever heard of a singin' nurse?"

Barbara shrugged. "There's worse ways of supplementing your grant," she pointed out.

"I was nursin' I was kep' too busy to go off gallivantin'. Free time, all we wanted to do was get to bed."

"I'll bet you did!" Barbara raised an eyebrow and grinned.

"*Alone*," Grandma added severely. Although she often used an earthy Jamaican vocabulary, she was quite prudish when it came to jokes.

"Things are different now, Gran," Barbara told her. "I'm an undergraduate with time to study. I don't have to run between ward and classroom at the beck and call of all and sundry."

"Seems to me you doin' plenty runnin' round between singin' and nursin'," observed Gran.

"Oh, I only do a bit of singing for Kenny," Barbara assured her. Though it wasn't true: she and Theo, her accompanist, now had regular Friday night bookings in the Medics' Mess at St Ag's.

"Huh!" Gran's grunt showed she knew better. "You want more toast?"

"Yes please – and more coffee." Barbara re-filled her cup. "You know, I do work hard at college, Gran – you've seen my results."

Grandma Robinson plopped two slices of bread into the toaster and then looked across the table at her grand-daughter. "I've seen them all right," she said. "You're doin' fine, Barbie-gal." Her smile beamed out, warm and loving. "I'm pleased and I'm proud – and so's your ma."

Barbara went round the table to hug her. For a moment they stood close, Gran resting her grey, fuzzy head against Barbara's shoulder. Surely she was getting smaller? thought Barbara. But then, it was easy to forget Gran Robinson had turned seventy now.

"Thank you, Grandma," she said. "That's praise indeed, coming from you."

Gran broke away and looked sternly up at her grand-daughter. "Just you keep it up, gal, that's all we ask," she said. "After all that wasted time…"

When she'd first left college, Barbara had been thrilled to be offered a training place with a big City firm, only to discover she was little more than a token Black, token woman and token office glamour girl. After three years of being patronized and passed over for promotion she'd succumbed to her mother's – and her grandmother's – ambitions for her, and turned to nursing.

"That wasn't wasted time, Gran," Barbara said now. She picked up her toast and went back to her coffee. "That experience in the City taught me a lot about management – and mismanagement." She spread butter very thickly on a slice of toast. "And that's where the brightest future lies now."

"But I thought you's trainin' to be a nurse, not a secretary, runnin' a office."

"Oh, I could be running a hospital, or a trust, or even a health authority – you can't do better than that, Gran."

Grandma Robinson looked serious.

"Yes, you can," she said, "You can do nursin'."

"Of course I can," Barbara agreed. "That's what I'm training for, and I'll do it a year or two. But after that – who knows? The NHS is my oyster!" She raised her cup in a toast.

"Well," said Grandma Robinson drily, "don't go eatin' it all at once – I'd like a bit of it left for my old age."

A bit was about all that would be left of the NHS by the time Grandma Robinson got old, Barbara reflected, as she sorted out her clothes for packing. Although, now she came to think of it, Gran must be already "old" – in years, at least. Well, who's counting? she grinned to herself. Go on for ever, Gran would, or at least long enough for her granddaughter to reorganize the NHS!

Not right now, though. She glanced around the room, collected a few things from her dressing-table, zipped up her weekend bag and set off downstairs.

"Barbara – am I glad to see you! Thought I'd miss you, gal!" Her mother stood in the tiny hallway. "I've just got time to give you a lift to Victoria."

"Oh, thanks, Ma, glad you made it. So it wasn't a boy then?"

"What?" Her mum looked puzzled.

"Gran said it must be a boy as it was taking so long," laughed Barbara.

"Might well be," her mum said. "Still on its way."

"Poor woman!" Barbara grimaced.

Her mother shrugged. "She's all right – no danger. Worse things than labour, gal. At least there's a reward at the end."

"Call a howling kid a reward?" Barbara reached for her jacket. "No thanks!"

"You go on thinking that way for a year or two yet," said her mother. "Come on – traffic's terrible. I think the sunshine's brought everyone out today."

Barbara paused at the kitchen door.

" 'Bye, Gran!" she called. "I'm off!"

"Not yet you're not – I haven't packed up your cookies."

"Come on, Gran," Barbara said impatiently. "Mum's waiting for me."

"Here you are, Barbie-gal!" Grandma Robinson handed over a foil-wrapped parcel. "Peanut," she said. "Your favourites!"

"Thanks, Grandma – you're too good to us all." Barbara bent to kiss the old lady.

"Yes, I know." Grandma Robinson beamed. "Now you go takin' care of yourself up there!"

"I will, Gran – and I'll share the cookies with the gang at Kelham's." Barbara balanced the parcel of cookies precariously in one hand and picked up her bag in the other. "And mind, you take care too – don't be cleaning and cooking all hours. Make Kenny take a turn." She laughed at the pained expression on Grandma Robinson's face. "See you in a few weeks' time – the end of my first year, would you believe!"

"And you just make sure you stick to your studyin'. None of that singin' till all hours, gal."

"No – not till all hours, Gran – see you!"

Barbara rushed along the hall to the open front door. She was about to dash down the steps when something prompted her to look back into the kitchen. Grandma Robinson stood, unaware she was being observed, leaning against the kitchen table, head bowed, as if praying. And she suddenly looked quite old and frail.

Barbara hesitated, then her mother gave a pip on the car horn. Well, perhaps Grandma Robinson was really praying, Barbara decided, probably for her safe journey back to Brassington – it was just the kind of thing she would do. Smiling to herself, she pushed the door to with her foot and ran down the steps.

"Sorry to keep you waiting. Gran insisted on packing some cookies. You'd think we never got fed at St Ag's!"

Her mother smiled. "It's not a case of being fed," she said. "It's just so's you remember her."

"I don't need a cookie to make me remember Gran," said Barbara. "I think of her every day."

"I'm glad you do." Serena Robinson leaned forward to check the road at the junction. "I'm a bit worried about her, you know," she said.

"Why?" asked Barbara, somewhat alarmed by this role reversal. Gran was the official worrier in the Robinson family: her son's failed marriage, her grandsons' peculiar jobs, her daughter-in-law's increasing work-load, her grand-daughter's career – all grist to Grandma Robinson's worrying mill. "Still missing Dad, is she?"

Her mother made a face. "I suppose," she said. "But I don't think that's at the root of it."

"Well, what is?" Barbara had a sudden vision of Grandma Robinson, as she'd just seen her, leaning heavily on the kitchen table. "She's not ill, is she?" she asked, anxiously.

"No, not ill – just not as well as she was. Didn't you notice? She sits around a lot more, dozes off, stays home a lot. Do you know, she's even been missing her church meetings!"

"Oh, Mum!" Barbara groaned. "You mean we're wearing her out? And I've just sat in the kitchen and let her feed me breakfast!"

"She'd enjoy that, love, don't you worry. Anyway, I'm taking her for a check-up this week – I'll let you know how she goes on. I dare say there's nothing wrong with her except getting older – and there's nothing anyone can do about that."

Which made it worse, Barbara reflected. She'd seen the effects of extreme old age on her current placement in geriatrics and she didn't like to think of Grandma Robinson getting like some of her patients. She sat in brooding silence until they approached Victoria coach station.

"Don't bother about parking," she told her mother. "Just pull in here. 'Bye, darling!" She gave her mother a quick peck on the cheek. "See you at the end of term!"

"End of your first year," said her mother happily. "Do well, my darlin'!"

"I will," Barbara promised.

And as she stood on the pavement, watching her mother's little car – courtesy of Community Nursing – disappear into the line of traffic, she wondered just what it was she would do well – nursing? Studying? Her exams? Oh yes, she'd do well in all of those, she was sure; she always did. But pushing her way through the crowded concourse, she thought again about the previous night, when she'd enjoyed herself so much and sung so well that Kenny was all for booking her again next weekend.

"You could do it," he'd told her. "Turn professional – now." He'd looked her up and down, critically. "You're at your peak," he said. "You're looking good and the voice is great. Leave it another year or so and you'll have blown it, Ba. Look – right now there's Rob with his programme, me with the band and you with the voice; the Robinsons are all set for success this year, man!"

And she'd smiled dismissively and told him not to hassle her.

"Think about it!" he'd insisted.

But she didn't really want to think about it. She had enough to think about, she reflected, settling into her seat on the north-bound coach: ward notes to copy up as soon as she got back, uniform to press ready for her placement next day, revision she'd promised herself she'd do every night...

Well, that was one thing she could do right now. Barbara reached into her bag, took out a medical textbook and settled down to read.

But all the time, behind the arid words of the text, she heard the insistent beat of music.

Chapter 2

Monday morning was always a tricky one in the Tinsdale unit: new patients to settle in; regulars returning for a spell of respite care to give their relatives a break; cars and ambulances, zimmers and wheelchairs, coming and going – it was more like an airport than a ward. The feeling of anxiety was almost palpable.

And today it was audible – expressed in strong, resonant tones and very commanding language.

"I was told to report here this morning," an old lady in a wheelchair was saying. "My housekeeper has gone off to Spain – says she needs a break, though I can't imagine why, she has little enough to do in my small flat. Then these lovely men came to collect me..." She tilted her head and flashed a wide smile at the ambulance man who'd wheeled her into the foyer. "I was assured there was a room booked…"

She sounded as if she were checking in at some luxury hotel – looked like it too, Barbara observed. The lady was dressed in a dark, flowing skirt and black velvet jacket with a multi-coloured shawl thrown over her shoulders. Her fine, white hair was cut short, shaped around her small, fine-boned face like a medieval pageboy's. She sat in her wheelchair, upright and elegant as a duchess, her brilliant dark eyes darting everywhere.

In contrast, Sister Tate looked pink and plump and flustered.

"Ach I'm rrreally sorry, Miss Wilde," she said in her soft Highland voice. "It's just that I don't seem to have your forms…"

"Oh, you don't need forms!" Miss Wilde waved a dismissive hand. "Just tell the man where my room is and I'll get out of your way. You can send someone to do my unpacking later – I can see you're very busy, dear."

Barbara almost laughed aloud. She couldn't believe this lady, here in an NHS hospital, talking to Sister as if she was some hotel receptionist. Who did this woman think she was?

"Ah, Barbara!" Sister Tate seized the opportunity to get away from Miss Wilde for a moment. "You were in the office, Friday afternoon?"

"Yes, I was working at the computer," Barbara agreed. She spent part of each day doing that: Tinsdale was always understaffed and admin. was not Sister Tate's favourite occupation.

"Did they not deliver the blue forms for this week? You know, the registration forms?" Sister Tate looked desperate.

"Not when I was there."

The ambulance man spoke. "Look Sister, I've got to get on – there's an ambulance full of folk out there…"

"Yes, all *rrright*!" Sister Tate nodded fiercely. "Barbara, take Miss Wilde to the Day Room – make her some coffee…" She looked pointedly at Barbara, who realized she meant "keep the old dear occupied while I find those damned forms."

"Certainly, Sister," she said cheerfully. "Come along, now, Miss Wilde, let's get you settled in…"

"You can hardly settle me in if you haven't found me a room," the old lady pointed out as Barbara pushed the wheelchair across the foyer.

"Well, we can settle into the Day Room, can't we?" said Barbara cheerfully.

"You can – I won't," returned Miss Wilde. "I just want to settle into my own room."

"It's not quite ready yet," Barbara soothed. Well, if the old girl insisted on treating the place as a hotel she could put up with the usual receptionist's response. "I'll make you a coffee and get you a magazine. By the time you've finished them we'll have something sorted."

"I want the *Telegraph*, not those silly magazines. And strong black coffee in a cup, not one of those poly-whatnot things that burn your fingers off."

Really, she was quite impossible, thought Barbara, pushing the wheelchair into the Day Room and placing it in front of the wide window which overlooked the hospital grounds.

"There! Isn't that beautiful?" she said, gazing across at the lake, cold blue in the sunshine, fringed by trees just bursting with fresh green.

Miss Wilde gave a cursory glance. "Empty," she said.

"What do you mean, empty?" asked Barbara. "Just look at all that space…"

"Exactly. Space is all there is. No people, no traffic, no shops, no streets – nothing happening."

Barbara looked out again. Actually, she'd often felt the same about the beautiful grounds at St Ag's. But everyone admired the landscaped park; whole committees sat agonizing about preserving it. Katie Harding, one of the Six who lived at Kelham House along with Barbara, had even organized a protest march when it was being suggested that the hospital building should be extended into the grounds. But privately, Barbara had always thought they were an extravagance – a luxury St Ag's couldn't afford now. And anyway, as Miss Wilde put it, they were empty.

"You should see the view from my flat," that lady was going on. "Straight on to the concourse above the shopping mall – never a dull moment!" She smiled, and Barbara thought again what a beautiful woman she was. Her finely wrinkled skin was like parchment, but it was stretched across good cheekbones, and her eyes were still large and dark, still lively with interest – and arrogance.

"Did you say something about coffee?" she asked sharply. "And a newspaper?"

"Certainly, Madam," smiled Barbara. "Though I don't think we have the *Telegraph*."

Barbara unearthed a copy of the *Guardian* from the staff common-room, made coffee in the single real cup reserved for consultants and was on her way to deliver them when Sister Tate came out of the office.

"How are you doing?" she asked anxiously.

"Fine," Barbara assured her. "Just delivering her comforts, and as soon as I've curtsied to Her Highness I'll be free!"

Unusually, Sister Tate didn't laugh.

"Look – could you do me a favour? You're a whizz on the computer…"

"Yes?"

"I'll take these things to Miss Wilde if you can call up this week's entrants' list. There's been a hold-up on the blue forms but they're all on disk – they say."

Without waiting for an answer, Sister Tate took the paper and the tray from Barbara and shot off down the corridor to the Day Room.

It didn't take Barbara long to bring up the weekly list and print off a copy. Miss Wilde was going to be disappointed, she noted: she was sharing Bay C with three other patients. The private rooms were all booked for post-ops. She went off in search of Sister Tate.

Guided by the sound of laughter, Barbara found her in the Day Room with Miss Wilde in full flow. Sister Tate had the gift of bringing the best out of her patients, Barbara reflected, as she stood at the door, reluctant to disturb the couple. Confused or weeping, disgruntled or downright rude, the old people always responded to Morag Tate's gentle Highland accent and her obvious concern for their welfare. Barbara often thought it was a pity she hadn't got the same magic touch in the office; it would have saved her a lot of hassle.

"Sister Tate, I've got the weekly list," she said, grasping a space in Miss Wilde's conversation.

"Have you? How clever!" Sister Tate beamed with delight. "Miss Wilde, Barbara Robinson's our student nurse. I think you've met?"

"We have," said Miss Wilde, nodding graciously. "Do I gather you've found me a room?"

"Well, your name's on the list," said Barbara. She handed the print-out to Sister Tate, not envying her the job of explaining to the formidable lady that she'd have to share an area of the ward.

"Ach, yes…" The Sister ran her finger down the list. "Heavens! What a lot of post-ops we have this week – and Mr Coulthard's away to Australia for a conference…" She looked a little apprehensively at Miss Wilde. "Well, now, let me see – you're in Bay C."

"Bay C?" Miss Wilde's head came up, like a temperamental horse sniffing the wind. "What does that mean?"

"It means you can have your choice of beds as you're the first arrival," said Sister Tate. "I should take the bed by the window – there's a lovely view over the lake." She smiled encouragement at her patient.

Miss Wilde merely stared at her. "What do you mean, 'the first arrival'?"

"Well, there will be other people in Bay C, but don't worry – you have your own alcove." Sister Tate smiled.

"*Alcove?*" The old lady said it as if it were a foreign word to her – and a dirty one at that. "Do you mean to say that I've been allocated an *alcove*?"

Barbara resisted the temptation to giggle; Miss Wilde's outrage was beautifully expressed – if a bit over the top, like an actress milking her best line.

"Well, yes, that's the usual arrangement," Sister Tate soothed. "The singles are all taken up with post-op patients this week." She stood up briskly, obviously anxious to get away from this demanding lady. "Now, Barbara will take you across to Bay C and help you sort out your things. I'll see you again at lunch…"

Clutching her list as if it were a life-line, Sister Tate made her getaway.

Well, thank you very much, Sister! thought Barbara.

"Right – we'll pick up your bags from reception on our way to Bay C," she said, flicking the brake off the wheelchair and turning it round.

"No, don't bother," Miss Wilde replied stiffly. "Just get that lovely ambulance man to take me back home."

Barbara paused, recognizing the set, stubborn tone. Grandma Robinson used it whenever things weren't going her way.

"I can't do that, I'm afraid," she said gently. "They won't take orders from a mere student."

"Then tell someone else to do it, child."

"I can't *tell* anyone to do anything. I'm here to learn and to observe, not to give orders – and, if you don't mind, I'm not a child." Barbara moved round so that she was facing the old lady.

"Nor you are." Miss Wilde looked her up and down. "A little old to be a student, aren't you?"

Barbara laughed. "I'm what they call a mature student," she explained. "I started my training late." She hesitated. "Look, I know you're disappointed about the room, but just let me take you over to see it. The bays are arranged like little apartments, with comfy chairs and low tables, and the bedroom areas are curtained off – you'll find it quite private."

"Sounds like some tin–pot boarding school," grumbled Miss Wilde.

"Oh, it's much more fun than that!" said Barbara. "You know, you'd be very lonely in a single room; nobody to chat to, no comings and goings to observe. If I were you," she bent over the wheelchair confidentially, "I'd choose the bed by the corridor – a bit noisier but much more going on…" She waited, hopefully, for a response.

Miss Wilde sniffed.

"Well, no harm in taking a look, is there?" she said. "Off you go!"

"Did you get the Duchess settled in?" asked Sister Tate later.

"Yes – all unpacked and established in her armchair," Barbara smiled.

"I'm so glad you managed it," said Sister. "I'd visions of her demanding to go home."

"Well, she did have that idea, but luckily, just as we arrived in Bay C, Mr Gough came bowling through and seemed to recognize her. You wouldn't believe the transformation that man made – she was positively flirtatious! They're planning on 'taking lunch' together, I believe."

"Are they, indeed? The forward old things!" Sister Tate laughed. "Well done, Barbara – I thought we were in for a scene with that formidable lady."

"Oh, I'm sure we are, when the others arrive in Bay C," said Barbara. "Perhaps we should put her in Bay B with Harold Gough!"

"Barbara, wash your mouth out!" said Sister Tate. "He's far too young for her."

"Well, he could be her toy boy!"

They were still laughing together when they became aware of someone hovering at the ever-open office door.

"Sister Tate?" he asked hesitantly.

Quelling the laughter, Sister Tate stood and drew herself as tall as her stocky figure would allow.

"That's me," she said. "Can I help you?"

"Dr Craster – taking Mr Coulthard's list."

"Oh yes, of course." Sister Tate moved back to her desk in a flurry of activity. Barbara, thinking it best to make a tactful retreat, turned to leave just as the doctor stepped into the tiny office, blocking the doorway. He was both tall and broad, Barbara noticed as she stood waiting for him to move.

"Excuse me," Barbara said, edging to her left.

"Certainly," said Dr Craster, edging to his right – and still blocking the way. So Barbara slid right and the doctor slid left and the doorway was still blocked.

This could go on for some time, thought Barbara, finding the idea not unappealing.

"Shall we dance?" she smiled. It was the kind of flippant remark the students made when they got into a jam in a corridor.

Dr Craster obviously didn't get it.

"Dance? What do you mean?" he said in a harsh accent she couldn't quite place – not quite Scottish but somewhere close, she thought. And somewhere rather lacking in humour, she reflected, feeling rather foolish after her flippant remark.

"Could you let me pass, please?" she said sweetly, as if to a small child.

"Gladly," he said, with an air of relief. He stood aside, pushing the door back with an air of ceremonial – like a flunkey at a ball.

"Thank you," said Barbara, resisting the temptation to add "kind sir!" But she couldn't resist glancing up as she passed him in the doorway, and for a moment her step faltered: his eyes, amazingly, fiercely blue, stared right through her. For once, Barbara was glad of her dark skin – at least it hid her blushes.

But why on earth should she blush? she asked herself as she shadowed Nurse Mark Hanson on drugs round later on. She wasn't the blushing type – never flustered, rarely embarrassed, always cool and calm, even before a gig. So why did Dr Craster make her blush? Good lord, he wasn't even her type! Red hair, pale skin, raw-boned – there was only his height in his favour. But then, those eyes! She shivered as she remembered the way he'd stared at her in the doorway.

No, he was actually glaring because of her awkwardness, she told herself. And then her joke had fallen flat – the bloke obviously had no sense of humour!

"You can take these over to Mr Gough," Mark was saying. He held out a little paper cup in which some pills were rattling. "Make sure he takes them, mind – don't just leave them for him. He has been known to hoard them."

"Of course," said Barbara sharply. She wasn't sure whether to be irritated or amused by Mark's patronizing attitude. After all, he had only just qualified – and was a year younger than herself. And inches shorter, she grinned, moving to his side to get the pills.

"That's all right," she smiled down at him. "He'll take them from me. Do anything for me, Harold Gough would!" She put a hand on her hip and sashayed away, swaying her hips in a provocative fashion as if she were off to seduce Harold, not just give him his pills. As Mark's appreciative laughter died away, she glanced back and gave a really sexy wink. Then she saw that Dr Craster had joined him.

Blushing fiercely and drawing herself up to her full height, Barbara walked majestically across to Harold Gough's bed. And all the time she was aware of Dr Craster's sharp blue eyes watching her.

Chapter 3

*Theo rang – asks you to get in touch – important!!!
K.*

Barbara smiled at the note she'd just picked up in her room. Trust Katie Harding to use three exclamation marks and turn a routine phone message into a drama! It was probably nothing very important – a new song, another booking. Theo had turned composer now as well as accompanist, and he had his sights set a lot higher than the Medics' Mess. He'd been filling in for an agency on gigs around the town and Barbara knew he was eagerly following up his contacts there.

"If we put the right programme together, get the right booking at the right club," he'd told her, "we could make it!"

"Make what?" she'd asked.

"Make a demo tape, a recording – a professional team."

She smiled and shook her head. "But we *are* professional," she'd said. "You're a doctor and eventually I'll be a nurse – highly respected professions both."

And Theo had groaned. "You sound just like my mother," he'd said. "Now just listen to this…"

And he'd played his latest song, mellow and sad and haunting. In spite of herself, Barbara had been impressed.

"Did you ring Theo?" Katie Harding asked over supper in the cafeteria.

Barbara shook her head. "Won't be home – you know what a junior houseman's life's like." She put her tray on the table and sat down. "Thanks for taking the message," she said. "Sounds like some real drama, eh?" She smiled at Katie.

"Yeah. Well, Theo certainly thought so – he was quite high," Katie said. "I was dying to know what it was all about, but he wouldn't tell me." She sounded quite aggrieved: Katie liked to know everything about everybody.

"Probably just some changes to the programme for Friday night," Barbara assured her.

"Oh, you're singing in the Medics' Mess again?" asked Claire Donovan. "That's great – we'll all come."

"Well, nobody's actually booked us yet, but you know what the committee's like – leave everything till the last minute."

"No we don't!" Katie, who was on every student committee in college, was quite indignant. "And anyway, Medics' Mess has its own committee – we don't run it."

"Ah, well, that accounts for it," Barbara grinned. "I'm sure if you were in charge you'd have gigs booked years ahead."

"I'd book you and Theo every Friday, that's for sure," Katie declared. "Anyone for pud?" She got up.

"Double ice-cream," said Jan Buczowski.

"Of course!" Katie bowed. "Chocolate sauce, sir?"

"Double sauce too."

They all laughed. Jan's appetite was legendary.

"I'll just have coffee," said Barbara. "Those lunches over at Tinsdale are so filling."

"I'll be making some fresh coffee back at Kelham's," Claire offered. "Come on, Barbara – we'll leave these two to pig away at their puddings."

"OK – and I'll ring Theo while you brew up."

But Theo still wasn't there. Barbara went back up to the kitchen and produced Grandma Robinson's peanut cookies to go with Claire's coffee, by which time the two pud-eaters had arrived. They all sat around the kitchen table in companionable silence, sipping coffee, nibbling biscuits, putting off what they all knew they should be doing – revision.

"The biscuit tin's almost empty," Jan commented, helping himself to another cookie.

"I'll refill it," Claire offered. "Another parcel from home, I'm afraid."

She sounded quite apologetic, and they all grinned at her. Claire's parents owned a country hotel out in Donegal and her father regularly bombarded the Kelhamites with parcels of luxuries – smoked wild salmon, hand-made chocolates, local cheeses…

"Oh – treats from Ireland!" said Jan happily. "So there will be plenty for all six of us." He held out the tin of cookies. "You may have another, Katie."

Katie shook her head and looked rather glum.

"'All six of us'," she repeated thoughtfully. "Remember when we were the famous Kelham Six?"

"In-famous, I rather think," said Jan.

"*In*fam-ous," Claire corrected. "That's how we say it. And anyway, I don't think we are."

"No – we're neither infamous nor six any more," said Katie. "Or hadn't you noticed?"

The others were silent. They all knew what Katie meant: the six top-floor Kelhamites had become great friends, bound together by their shared kitchen – and shared struggles in their first year of training. And there were still six of them up at the top of the house: Katie Harding, Barbara Robinson, Claire Donovan, Jan Buczowski, Nick Bone and Nikki Browne, but these days only four of them met regularly; Nick and Nikki had become an item and rarely joined the others in the cafeteria or up in the kitchen.

"Then there were four," Barbara grinned. "Well, it was bound to happen sometime – we all move on."

"And we all move out very soon," said Claire.

Jan looked startled. "What do you mean?"

"Top floor Kelham's is always reserved for first-years," Claire explained. "We're going to be seconds next term."

"And so we have to move out?" Jan asked, his voice filled with anxiety.

"Or down," Barbara soothed. "We can take the rooms on the first floor."

"And for the third year we live in the garden, I think?" Jan smiled bleakly.

The girls laughed, though Barbara noticed Jan didn't join in. He still got upset at the thought of change, she realized. Poor Jan! A refugee from war-torn Central Europe, he'd had too many changes in the past couple of years.

"For the third year we live out," she told him gently. "Maybe we could all share a house?"

"Never mind the third year," said Katie. "What are we going to do in our second?"

Barbara shrugged. "Move downstairs, I suppose."

"But that's divided into two self-contained flats," said Claire.

"Each with three beds – quite enough for the six of us," Barbara smiled.

But Claire didn't. "That means three sharing," she pointed out. "And we all know three's a crowd."

"Anyway, there's not six of us just now." Katie looked gloomily into her coffee mug. "I reckon those two will set up home together next year."

Barbara was shocked. "But it's much cheaper to live in," she said. "I wouldn't have thought Nikki can afford it, with all the extra bills…"

"No, but Nick could afford it for both of them," Claire pointed out. "He's never short of money."

"Has he said anything to you?" Barbara turned to Jan.

Jan shrugged. "He is older than us, you know. Maybe he needs a place of his own."

"He's only as old as Barbara," Katie pointed out. "And she's quite content with us, aren't you, Barbara?"

"Darlings, I love you all!" Barbara flung out her arms in a theatrical gesture and gave a toothy smile. "But I'm not going to worry about next year until this year's over," she said, dropping the pose and looking sternly round the table. "And you all know what comes before that!"

"Exams!" everyone groaned.

"Right," agreed Barbara. "So I suggest we all

adjourn to our rooms and get a bit of work done – OK?"

"Certainly, Aunty Babs," said Jan. "We will all take your advice. Come on, Claire – I'll test you on the physiology papers!"

I wish they wouldn't call me "Aunty Babs", Barbara thought, as she sat at her desk later. One of these days they'll find me out!

The name had been invented by Nick Bone, on account of everyone's habit of turning to Barbara for help and advice. It wasn't just a matter of age – she was more mature, more streetwise, than the others, and coming from a nursing family she knew a lot more about the profession than they did. So "Aunty Babs" she became, although she didn't feel any older or wiser than the rest of them.

She smiled to herself, suddenly remembering her gran's words.

"'S time you grew up, Barbie-gal," she'd say, if she knew Barbara had been off clubbing with her friends. "'S oright them boys playin' aroun' – they's a long time growin'. Sometimes not at all." And she'd sniff her disapproval at all things male. "Women's got important work to do, Barbie. Sooner you realize that, the better."

Funny that, she thought. Gran treated her like a ten-year-old, her friends at St Ag's treated her like an agony aunt, and all the time she felt like – what?

Barbara shrugged. Like any twenty-something, she'd guess: part teenager, clubbing and dancing all night long; part mature adult, gazing cool and long-term into the future. Her future, Ms Barbara Robinson B.Sc. RGN Dip.Inst.Acc. Chief Executive, Sometown Hospital Trust…

"Ba! Phone!" Claire called along the corridor. "Theo again, I'll bet!"

But it wasn't Theo. It was her brother, Rob.

"Rob – what's wrong?" Rob never rang, never wrote, was rarely at home when she was there – they hadn't spoken together for months. She had a sudden premonition. "Is it Grandma?"

"How'd you guess?"

"Never mind – tell me what's happened. Is she all right?"

"Yeah, she's all right – now."

"What do you mean 'now'?" Barbara shut her eyes, gritted her teeth; Rob's laid-back attitude had always grated on her. "Come on, Robbie, for good-ness' sake!"

"Seems she had a fall. Ma asked me to ring – she's at the hospital with her now…"

"When did it happen? Was she at home?"

"This afternoon, down the market – she must've slipped on stuff. You know those pavements, never cleaned up till the market's closed. Anyway, she was whipped off to Casualty and they called Ma – lucky she was in a meeting not the delivery room, eh?"

He sent his intimate DJ chuckle down the line but it only added to her irritation.

"So what has Gran done – broken something?"

"Nah, nothing broken, just freaked out, I guess. Ma asked me to pass on the message. Didn't want you ringing home and finding nobody there – you know how she is," he ended easily.

"I know how *we* are," she told him grimly. "Gran and Ma, Kenny and me. We keep in touch, Rob, we communicate – you know?" She knew she was getting shrill so she paused and took a deep breath. "Now, you tell me: if there's nothing wrong why did Ma ring you of all people? And why aren't they sending Grandma home already?"

"Chill it, Ba! How do I know? You know hospitals – tell you nothing. They're keeping her in for observation, that's all Ma said. Oh – and not to ring the hospital. She'll bell you some time, give you all the medical stuff, I expect. OK? Stay tuned, man!" He gave his usual radio farewell.

"Wait!" Barbara almost screamed at him. But the line went dead – Rob had signed off.

Shaken, Barbara made her way along the corridor to her room, changed her mind and looked in the kitchen, feeling the need for coffee.

Claire Donovan was stacking the fridge.

"I'm taking up all the space again," she apologized. "You'll be helping yourselves, I hope." She closed the door and turned. "You all right, Barbara?" she said.

"You look – er – well, quite pale."

For once, Barbara didn't take up the obvious joke. She went over to the sink, filled the kettle and then stood, looking blankly round as if she'd forgotten what she was going to do with it.

"Here – I'll do that. You sit down." Claire gently took the kettle from her, plugged it in and ushered her to a chair. "Is it coffee you're wanting?" she asked.

Barbara merely nodded.

In silence, Claire made two mugs of coffee – instant this time, though she usually scorned such stuff.

"There you are," she said, pushing one across the table to Barbara. "Now, are you going to tell me what's wrong? Is it your old ladies up in Tinsdale?"

Barbara gave a slight smile at the idea of Grandma Robinson being one of her "old ladies".

"Not one up in Tinsdale," she said. "It's my grandma – she's in hospital."

"Oh no!" Claire was quick to sympathize. They all knew about Grandma Robinson up at Kelham's. She was their regular supplier, via Barbara, of spicy cookies, sound advice and hilarious stories. None of the gang had ever met her, but everyone felt she was part of the family. "Is it serious?" Claire asked.

Barbara groaned. "I don't know," she said. "That's the trouble. That brother of mine is so laid-back he'd keep his cool if his coat was on fire!"

"Your brother the DJ?"

Barbara nodded. "Ma left him to pass the news on to me – she's at the hospital with Grandma. And would you believe – he's in radio, for God's sake, but he can't even communicate a bit of family news coherently! Sounded as if he were doing a programme!" Barbara picked up her coffee and took a gulp.

"Well, you know families," said Claire wisely. "Never tell you all the details – assume you get them by some process of osmosis." She smiled and put a hand on Barbara's arm. "I'm sure if it were anything serious he'd have told you."

"Yes, of course he would." Barbara sounded as if she were trying to convince herself.

"Did she have a fall?" Claire asked.

"Yes – out on the street apparently."

"And has she broken anything?"

"Oh no – nothing broken, Rob said."

"Well, then, there you are!" Claire beamed encouragingly.

"Yes, but where?" asked Barbara, thinking aloud. "If it's not serious why did Ma ring Rob of all people? I mean, we never ring Rob – he's difficult to talk to even when you're in the same room; on the phone he's impossible."

"Well, he did pass the message on," Claire pointed out.

"Yeah." Barbara sighed, feeling suddenly

exhausted. "Yeah, he did that at least. But he said they were keeping her in for observation – now why would they do that?"

"To keep an eye on her," smiled Claire. "That's nothing sinister, is it? An old lady falling on the street. She might have some delayed concussion, perhaps."

The diagnosis sounded reasonable and Barbara longed to believe it.

"But my mother's a nurse, and beds are worth their weight in gold in London," she said.

"You could ring the hospital," Claire suggested.

Barbara shook her head. "Ma said not to – she's neurotic about not using family influence. Said she'll ring me later."

"Well, of course she will," Claire said. "As soon as she sees your grandma settled she'll get herself home and ring, and then you'll get all the details."

"Yeah, you're right, of course." Barbara took a deep breath. "Thanks, Claire – it's good to have somebody talking sense after listening to Rob."

Claire laughed. "Well, lots of people seem to like listening to Rob – he can't be that bad!"

"Don't you believe it," Barbara smiled. "Anyway, I feel straighter in my mind now. Thanks for the coffee, love – and for listening to my moans."

"Not at all!" Claire assured her. "How often have you listened to us all, in this kitchen, moaning away, waiting for Aunty Babs to help us?" She stood up.

"It's high time we helped Aunty Babs a bit," she said. "I'll give you a shout if there's a call for you this evening." Claire's room was closer to the phone than Barbara's.

"Thanks, Claire, but aren't you revising with Jan?"

Claire shook her head. "We've finished," she said softly. "He's gone down to the basement to play his fiddle."

Barbara looked closely at her. They both knew what that meant: Jan was feeling homesick, distancing himself from his work, his friends – even from Claire.

The two girls stood for a moment, exchanging sympathetic looks. Suddenly Barbara moved closer and hugged Claire. For a second they stood by the table, dark skin against pale, sleek hard head above tangled wild one.

"He'll be all right," said Barbara.

"And so will your gran," murmured Claire.

They stood back, smiling.

"I'm going to get myself ready for bed," said Barbara, breaking away. "Hard day tomorrow!" She smiled, rather shakily.

"I'll listen out for the phone," Claire promised. "I've a load of reading to do."

"Good night, then, Claire – and thanks!"

"Good night, Ba," Claire smiled. "Try not to worry."

But how could she not worry? Barbara asked herself as she undressed, when her beloved grandma was lying alone in a hospital bed? And she suddenly remembered her last glimpse of her in the kitchen at home, bowed over the table, looking somehow small and frail. Maybe she'd been feeling ill at that very moment, waiting for a pain to subside, perhaps, or feeling faint?

Then her mother had said how worried she was. And something about her being tired, not going out so much. Could that have anything to do with her fall? Had she collapsed? Had a heart attack?

Of course not, Barbara told herself. If that was the case Grandma Robinson would be in Intensive Care and she, Barbara, would be on the next train to London. Be sensible, she chided herself. "Nothing serious," Rob had assured her. All she had to do was to wait for the next bit of news. Barbara slipped into her purple dressing gown – one of her father's extravagant parting gifts – and stretched out on the bed. Waiting was harder than working, she reflected, so she picked up her anatomy book and tried to read. Within minutes she was asleep.

Chapter 4

Barbara sped through the grey drizzle as lightly as if she were dancing in tropical sunshine. When Ma finally had rung, late last night, it was to tell her that Grandma Robinson seemed to be all right and they were just waiting for the results of her tests.

"I'll ring you tomorrow evening, when I hope to have some more news. Good night, darlin'. Sleep tight!"

And, much relieved, Barbara had slept tight – and late. Now she was racing across the hospital grounds to Tinsdale, trying desperately to make up time. It would be too annoying if she lost marks for unpunctuality on this placement, when she'd got straight A's for all her others. She took a deep breath, clutched her navy blue cloak around her, and ran, head down, towards the entrance to Tinsdale.

She didn't see the short man with a white coat and a mop of curling black hair until she almost knocked him over. For a moment they stood, catching their breath and holding on to each other.

"Ba! I've been trying to catch you!" Theo said, shaking raindrops out of his bushy hair.

"Looks as if you've succeeded," Barbara laughed. "Mind out – I'm drenched!" She stepped away from him. "'Raindrops are falling off my head!'" she warbled.

"Sorry!" he said, wiping his glasses on the edge of his white coat. "Look – I must talk to you – I've had the most amazing—"

"Not now, Theo – I'm going to be late."

"Oh, I don't think Sister Tate will penalize you. You're obviously her star student."

"Am I?"

"Oh, yes. She's very impressed with your computer skills."

Barbara groaned. "It's my nursing skills she'll be reporting on," she said. "Computer skills don't count."

"But making a good impression on Sister does," he smiled.

"Maybe, but I won't be doing that if I turn up late. Sorry, Theo, I must go." Barbara shrugged her cloak from her shoulders and shook it, all ready to enter the ward.

"And we must talk, Ba," Theo said. "How about lunch?"

She hesitated. "Neither of us is likely to get away," she pointed out. "Is it about Friday?"

"And more, lots more. Look – I'll come round to Kelham's as soon as I get off duty this evening, all right?"

She'd be sitting waiting for her mother's next call, Barbara reflected. "I'll be in the common room – see you there!"

She turned and walked demurely into the foyer.

The foyer had the usual air of a departure lounge, though in the case of Tinsdale, it was full of arrivals. Without waiting to be told, Barbara took hold of a wheelchair and set off to the Day Room with her patient.

"Could you settle all the day folk in, Barbara?" Mark Hanson was already there, closing windows, arranging chairs in friendly groups, distributing pillows and rugs. "I've got a few pre-meds to do."

"Sure. I'll take all the ambulance arrivals."

The next half-hour was filled with welcoming day patients and trundling wheelchairs, walking-frames and, occasionally, a patient or two, until the Day Room filled up with quiet chatter and muted groans.

"The auxiliaries will be here with the trolley soon," Barbara announced. "I'm sure you're ready for a hot drink after your journey."

"The usual agonizing choice between tepid tea and feeble coffee, I suppose?" The cultured, resonant voice came from the corner which Evie Wilde had made her own.

"Hello, Miss Wilde." Barbara went over to her. "Why don't you come over and meet a few people?"

"Thank you, no; I've met some," Evie Wilde replied dismissively. "I'm waiting for a telephone call, but where's my telephone?" She glared at Barbara, who was minded to tell the lady to go private if she wanted such luxuries as a telephone of her own.

"Sister Tate will pass on any messages that come in," she said curtly.

Evie Wilde stared up at her. "But I want to speak to my caller myself."

"That's rather difficult unless you call them," Barbara said. Then she added, in her best soothing tone, "Look, I'll bring the trolley over as soon as we've got everyone settled, all right?"

"I suppose it will have to be," said Evie grudgingly. Suppressing her irritation, Barbara flashed a brilliant smile and left her.

On the ward, Barbara noted temperatures and blood pressures, turned immobilized patients, rubbed stiff and sore limbs, brought fresh pillows and tucked up legs, feeling that by working hard on Tinsdale Ward she was somehow nursing Grandma Robinson by proxy. Quite illogical, she told herself, but nevertheless it eased her mind a little.

She was even singing a little tune of Theo's when she finally got round to pushing the telephone trolley over to Evie Wilde.

"That's a nice little voice you have there, my dear," said Miss Wilde, in her patronizing way.

Barbara swallowed the urge to belt out a heavy rock number right in the old lady's ear. "Nice little voice" indeed!

"I've brought you the telephone," she said coolly.

"Ah well – the moment's passed," Miss Wilde said airily, and Barbara realized she'd forgotten all about taking or making a call: there probably never was one. Damn! After all the time and effort she'd spent getting the wretched thing over to her.

"Right!" she said briskly, turning the trolley round. "I'll take this back then."

"Oh, just leave it there, whatever it is," Miss Wilde ordered. "Now, what was the song you were singing?"

"Oh – just a little something someone wrote specially for me," Barbara replied casually. That'd show the old girl – "little voice" indeed!

The old girl was, indeed, impressed. "Wrote for you? What do you mean?" she asked.

"My accompanist…" Barbara paused, uncertain whether Evie was following.

"Yes, yes, go on – I know all about accompanists. Strange breed…"

How could she know? Barbara wondered. "Well, Theo often writes his own songs, for me to sing."

"Where?"

"Well, wherever we're asked. Fridays we're often booked for the Medics' Mess – the staff club, you know."

"So you're professionals?" For the first time since they'd met, Evie Wilde looked at Barbara with something like respect.

"Oh, yes – professional medics," Barbara laughed. "Theo's a doctor, you see."

But Evie Wilde had lost interest; she was singing softly to herself, lost in thought.

"… *a garden of Eden, just made for two…*"

Her voice, though slight and tremulous, was beautifully modulated and right on key. Barbara recognized the years of training behind that sound.

"Ah, you're the professional, Evie, aren't you?"

The old lady broke off singing and looked up now, her eyes clouded.

"Professional?" she repeated vaguely. Then, suddenly, on a burst of energy, she broke out, "*Alhambra, Lyceum, Hippodrome…*"

For a moment Barbara thought she was suffering from dementia, but as Miss Wilde went on reciting, "*The Royal, The Grand, The Palace…*" Barbara realized she was repeating names of theatres.

47

"Ah, I see now," she smiled. "You were an actress, were you?"

"Actress?" Evie Wilde looked shocked. "My dear, I was a *star*!"

"I'll bet you were," said Barbara, looking at the still beautiful face, the fine eyes, the tiny erect figure.

"A star of the musical theatre: revue, cabaret, musical comedy…" Evie continued. "I could teach you a thing or two about singing," she ended, glaring up at Barbara.

"I'd love to hear some of your songs," said Barbara.

Evie tilted her head, licked her lips as if to gloss them, and gave Barbara a brilliant, professional smile. "I can't possibly remember them all," she said, "but I'll work on one or two for you."

"I look forward to hearing them," Barbara assured her. "Meantime, duty calls. I'll leave you to rehearse your words – right?"

Miss Wilde nodded and waved a dismissive hand. Barbara pushed the trolley back through the day room and paused at the door to look back. There, in her corner, sat Miss Wilde, not glaring around as usual, but deep in thought, muttering gently to herself.

Rehearsing, thought Barbara, who'd often learned a new song in just the same way, travelling on the tube, sitting at her desk. Well, at least the old lady looked quite content, for once.

* * *

Kelham House was unusually silent at seven o'clock in the evening, Barbara realized. The rest of the Six – or was it only four now, as Katie insisted? – would all be over in the cafeteria, and the second-years were being treated to an open lecture, poor things! She settled herself on the common-room sofa, stretching out her long legs and bare feet in front of her, trying to relax and revise at one and the same time.

But it wasn't easy, with one ear listening for her mother's phone call and the other on alert ready for Theo's buzz at the door. Barbara hummed his latest song to herself and suddenly remembered her conversation with Miss Wilde. Who was she? she wondered. She'd never heard of a star of that name. But then, she wouldn't, would she? When Miss Wilde was trilling her way around English theatres, the Robinsons were gospelling around Jamaican churches. Barbara smiled at the idea. A pity she couldn't introduce Grandma to Evie Wilde – they'd have a lot in common, those two. The thought of Grandma Robinson started her worrying again. Why were the test results taking so long? And what were they going to reveal?

When the knock came on the door she jumped nervously.

"Oh – it's you, Barbara!" Sister Thomas smiled. "I saw the light was on – thought it was those careless second-years forgetting it again. I'm sorry if I disturbed you." She hesitated. "Everything all right?"

"Oh – yes. I'm just waiting to answer both the phone and the front door," Barbara said. "And I'm trying to do a bit of revision as well."

"You're never one to waste time," Sister Thomas observed. "I'm getting good reports of your work over at Tinsdale."

"Are you? Well, that's one less worry, I suppose."

"But you have others?" Sister Thomas came across the room and sat down. "Want to tell me about them?" she asked.

And suddenly Barbara felt the need to confide in someone, though she wasn't quite sure that Ann Thomas was the right person to listen to her worries about the singing career. So she told her all about Grandma Robinson's accident.

"...I can't see why they're keeping her in if she's just shook up after a minor fall," she finished.

"Well, I think they're being careful. She may not have slipped, she could have had a brief black-out and they need to ensure she won't be having any more," Sister Thomas suggested.

"Yes, that's what my mother says," Barbara agreed. "But surely those tests are fairly routine? On Tinsdale we'd have had the results within twenty-four hours."

"Ah, well, you have to realize that Tinsdale is a very special geriatric unit. Sister Tate prides herself on her high standards."

Immediately Barbara felt a surge of relief. Of

course! Brixton General wasn't a teaching hospital and Grandma's tests had probably gone off to some outside laboratory.

"You're right, Sister," she said. "Thank you – you've put my mind at rest."

"All part of the service!" said Sister Thomas. "It's easy to get things out of perspective when you're away from home." She waited for a moment, then went on, "If there's anything I can do to help, you know where my door is."

"I do," Barbara smiled. "But I should think Grandma will be home by the weekend. I'll be able to talk to her then."

"You're going home?" Sister Thomas was surprised. At the end of placement, the following week, there'd be an intense period of debriefing, final lectures, revision and exams – the climax of the whole year!

"No." Barbara shook her head. "I can't afford either the fare or the time."

But even as she spoke she was working out a plan. If Theo had news of another gig, she might be able to afford a coach ticket the following weekend – even pick up another gig with Kenny then...

Her plans were interrupted by a buzzing in the hall.

"I'll answer that." Sister Thomas got up. "I expect it's your visitor."

"Theo Britner – you know him," said Barbara.

"Ah! Your brilliant accompanist," Sister Thomas nodded. "More work, Barbara?" Her voice held a hint of disapproval. This was no time to be rehearsing songs.

"No, just a little meeting, I think," smiled Barbara.

I hope, she added to herself, as she heard Ann Thomas greeting Theo in the hall.

Then Theo, looking more dishevelled than ever, peered round the door.

"I'm late!" he announced. "But you know how it is…"

"I do," she agreed. "But do you know how hungry I am?"

Theo groaned. "Me too," he agreed.

"Well, hang on. I'll slip my shoes on and we'll go over to the cafeteria." She led the way back into the common room.

"Well, actually…" said Theo, and stopped.

"Actually what?" asked Barbara, bending over to pull on a pair of flat loafers.

"We need somewhere quiet – to talk. I've got things to tell you, private things…"

"You have? Wow! Exciting, huh?" Barbara was always teasing Theo about his hesitant manner. She looked at him now, rumpled and crumpled, his hair quite wild. Even his glasses were crooked. It was difficult to see Theo in a position of authority, either as a doctor or as a performer. "Where shall we go, then?" she asked.

"How about a Balti?" he suggested. "There's a new place down the road."

Now it was Barbara's turn to hesitate. She had some money from last weekend's gig, but then, she might need that for train fare…

"My treat," Theo offered.

"Oh now – that's not fair," she protested. A Junior Houseman didn't earn a great deal either.

"No – really – it's all right," Theo assured her. "I mean, you missed your supper on my account … and anyway, it's a sort of celebration…"

"What sort?" Barbara asked.

"Never you mind." Theo tapped the side of his nose. "I'll tell you over supper. Come on!"

Before they left Barbara rang home, but there was no reply. Presumably her mother was at the hospital, either on duty or visiting Grandma Robinson – probably both, knowing her mother! Promising herself she'd ring as soon as she got back, she joined Theo and together they walked down the road to the new restaurant.

"…so you see, it's going to mean a far bigger commitment," Theo told her over supper.

Barbara leaned back from the table, taking in the sweet, pungent scent of her Balti lamb – and the implications of Theo's news: the chance of a regular spot in a club in town and the opportunity to make a professional demo tape.

"But we don't have any time," she protested. "I've got exams coming up, you hardly have time to eat, never mind rehearse new stuff…"

"I know, I know!" Theo gloomily mopped up the rich sauce from his plate with flat naan bread. "But I could make time. I often stay on extra when legally I could leave…"

"Oh, legally!" Barbara swept hospital rules of employment away with a wave of her hand. "You and I know what we should do legally – and we both know we have to do lots more if the system is to work at all."

"Only if we want to stay within the system." Theo put down his fork and looked steadily at Barbara.

She stared back at him for a full, thoughtful moment.

"Well, I don't know about you, Theo," she said eventually, "but I have to stay within the system – at least until I'm qualified."

"Yes, I have to do the same, but that doesn't mean to say I can't have a private life as well. Good lord! Half my year are married, some even have kids…"

"Yes, and how often do they see them?"

"That's not the point. They take all their off-time to the very minute, never work over, live out – at least weekends – it's the single blokes who do all the filling in, extra hours, whatever. I could back off, treat my music like a wife."

"And we all know wives come a poor second to medicine," Barbara grinned. "I'd never marry a doctor."

Theo smiled at her knowingly.

"Or a musician," she added more pointedly.

"Now that you've spurned me on both counts..." Theo smiled, totally unperturbed. He'd never harboured romantic ideas about Barbara; she was too useful to his musical career. "What about this job?"

Barbara chewed her lip thoughtfully. "Wednesday nights, you say? Well, I could work round that. Even if we keep up our Fridays in the Medics' Mess that's only a couple of nights a week..." She was aware that she was persuading herself as well as Theo. It would be great to sing in a real club, to have a regular booking, try out Theo's new music...

"And the money's good," Theo reminded her.

"Yeah, I could certainly use some of that." But that wasn't the point and she knew it. Barbara had a sudden feeling of being pulled in two directions:

"*Time you gave up all that singin' nonsense!*" Grandma Robinson's voice.

"*You could go professional...*" Kenny had told her.

She shook her head, clearing the voices away, and looked at Theo.

"Well, go ahead with the club contract. I'm with you on that."

"And the demo tape?"

She shrugged. "I'm not setting anything off at half-cock," she said. "If we get a good session together, work it up to professional standard – well, then we'll do the tape, though how we'd ever find a free day together when the studio could take us..."

"You leave that to me, Ba." Theo leaned over and grasped her hand. "Hey! This could be the start of something really big, you know." He looked at her closely, his pale eyes sparkling behind metal glasses, his wide, thin mouth stretched into a grin.

"Don't hold your breath," warned Barbara, removing her hand gently and sitting back in her chair. "A minor gig in a small club in mid-week is hardly the big time, boy." And part of her hoped it never would be, she reflected.

"No, but it's a beginning," said Theo. "This girl who wants us to make a tape – she's an agent – she can push us on..."

"Hey, leave it out!" Barbara was suddenly alarmed. "One thing at a time. Wednesday's at Chuzzlewit's OK. Agents – no way. What I earn I intend to keep, right?"

"All right," Theo soothed. "We'll go ahead with the gig – for starters."

"Starting's what I should be doing now – starting on some revision," said Barbara, collecting her jacket and bag. "Shall we go?"

Chapter 5

After Theo's news, her phone call home, and, possibly, the spicy food, Barbara found it difficult to get to sleep that night. It couldn't be the food, she decided: any stomach reared on Grandma Robinson's chillies 'n' chicken couldn't object to Eastern spices. And although Theo was obviously excited by the prospect of the new gigs, she was not; after all, she'd done bigger gigs than Chuzzlewit's back in London with Kenny. No, what was spinning round and round in her head was her conversation with her mother.

She'd finally run her to ground at about ten o'clock.

"Ma? Where on earth have you been?" Barbara could hear the sharp edge in her voice. Well, no wonder. It was the third time she'd rung in the past hour.

"At the hospital, girl. Where d'you think?" Her mother, too, sounded quite cross.

"With Grandma or on duty?"

"Bit of both."

Ma sounded exhausted. "So – how is she?" Barbara asked, and was alarmed by her mother's hesitation.

"She's – all right," she said eventually.

"You don't sound too sure."

"Well, they still haven't got all the test results."

"But what's holding them up? I mean, there's nothing complicated, is there? She only fell down, after all."

"Question is, why?"

"Well, I thought Rob said she tripped, fell over something."

"No, seems she had a dizzy spell. Been having them for months. Told nobody, of course. Then this one took her in the middle of the market and so everybody knew – except her family."

To Barbara's surprise her mother's voice broke and for a second or two she sounded quite tearful.

"Ma, that's not your fault. She should have told you about them."

"No, she wouldn't do that. You know how much I depend on her to keep the household going. She's always been more than a mother-in-law to me, especially since your father left." Barbara heard her mother taking a deep, shaky breath. "It *is* my fault – it's the whole family's fault. We should have realized she's getting to be an old lady now, needing looking after, not looking after all of us…"

"She would hate that," Barbara pointed out. "And these dizzy spells, they could be something quite easily controlled – blood pressure, diabetes, poor circulation."

"That's my nursing girl!" Ma laughed a little. "Well, I guess they've ruled out all those simple things and we'll just have to wait for the rest of the results now."

"But they're keeping her in?"

"Yes. And I feel terrible about that. She could have come home if I were there all day. You know how she feels about leaving her bed."

"Yes," Barbara smiled. "And I'll bet she's just about running that ward now."

"Well, that's the strange thing. She isn't. For one thing there's no ward to run – it's more than half empty and very depressing. She's just lying back and taking no interest in anything."

"Tranks?"

"Of course not. She's only on a low-dose beta-blocker – to stabilize the blood pressure. They wouldn't make her so lethargic."

Barbara didn't know what to say. Lethargy was simply not part of Grandma Robinson's personality.

When the whole household was laid low with virulent 'flu one winter, she was the one who kept going. When she sprained her ankle in the garden she sat up all night plastering it with hot-and-cold compresses and was on her feet next morning, limping slightly but dishing up sweet fries as usual. When her favourite son, Errol, Barbara's father, split from the family and went to Jamaica, she buried her pain in work.

"Long as you workin', you's livin'," she'd say, a little grimly at that time. So she bustled around, intent on cheering Robbie, who'd wanted to go back with his dad, comforting Barbara and Kenny, who missed him dreadfully, and keeping things going for their mother, Serena, who was as dear to her as her own daughter.

"Maybe she's enjoying the rest," Barbara suggested lamely, and was rewarded with a scornful explosion from the other end of the line.

"Rest? Emmelia Robinson doesn't recognize the word – unless you're referring to the sacred eight-hours sleep, strictly during night-time hours."

Now Barbara really did laugh.

"Come on, Ma! Make yourself a nice drink, have a lovely hot bath and get your sacred eight hours. You'll feel more positive about all this in the morning."

"That's your prescription, is it?"

"Yes, it is."

"Well, you're right, Barbie. Thank goodness we're getting another medic in the family! Good night, darling!"

"Good night, Mum. Keep in touch."

"Of course. I'll ring as soon as we hear anything. God bless you, love."

"Good night. God bless."

Barbara had put down the phone and made her way back to her room, feeling utterly exhausted.

Yet now it was well past midnight and she hadn't been able to sleep. Oh, Lord! And she was going to follow Dr Craster's ward round in the morning. He was sure to ask her all kinds of penetrating questions. Maybe she should read over her ward notes…

"…the foundation of good nursing for the elderly, Student Nurse Robinson?" Dr Craster asked.

Barbara suppressed a yawn and blinked in the bright sunlight of the ward. "Er … sorry, I didn't quite hear," she said.

He gave her a penetrating look. "I was just saying that, medication apart, there are some good natural therapies we can use with elderly people. Can you give us an example?"

There was a pause as Barbara frantically tried to pull her thoughts together. "Natural remedies," he'd said. What was he thinking of – sensual massage? Herb tea?

"I notice you are in the habit of applying a natural therapeutic method yourself," he prompted.

"I am?" Barbara's brilliant eyes opened wide in surprise.

"Yes, you seem to have used it to win over one of our more difficult patients – Miss Wilde."

"Well, I've only been talking to her a few times," she said defensively.

"Exactly!" Dr Craster nodded vigorously. "Talking's the best therapy for the confused elderly, especially when they're away from familiar scenes."

Barbara breathed a sigh of relief – she'd got through that quite nicely! But Dr Craster obviously hadn't finished with her yet.

"What would you say are the special requirements for nursing in this department, SN Robinson?"

Barbara, who had never been called SN Robinson before, almost leapt to attention.

"Well…" she began. And the sleepless hours of the night before suddenly proved themselves useful. "A combination of things: physical strength for a start – no use coming here with a creaky back, we're already treating several; then there's patience, of course, but more than that – persistence, to help people rehabilitate after treatment or injury; and compassion for those who will never get any better." Dr Craster was looking at her expectantly, as if he knew she had more to say. So she took a deep breath and went on.

"In an odd way, geriatrics is like paediatrics – the patients need company, conversation, entertainment, as well as medication. Something to take their mind off their own disabilities, something to stimulate them…" Barbara's voice faded. She had a sudden vision of Grandma Robinson lying passive, lethargic, utterly unstimulated, in a hospital bed in a half-empty ward.

Dr Craster was still watching her closely. "Thank you, SN Robinson – a very comprehensive answer." He smiled at her, lifted a hand slightly as if in greeting and moved off down the ward.

Barbara was about to join his entourage when Sister Tate turned to her.

"Would you like to take your break now, Barbara? I'm sure you're ready for a coffee after that." She looked at her shrewdly. "You all right?" she asked.

"Oh yes – just in a bit of a whirl. Doctor's questions always feel like an exam, don't they?"

Sister Tate smiled. "Which in a way they are," she agreed. "But I don't think there's any doubt about the outcome of that little test – you passed with flying colours."

Barbara blushed. "Thank you very much, Sister Tate," she said.

"Not at all. You deserve it, Barbara. And I'm not just saying that because I need a favour." Sister Tate smiled. "Could you bear to do a little job in the office? There's a new drugs lists needs entering on to the computer and we've no admin. help for the next couple of days."

"Of course," Barbara assured her. "I'll get on to it right away."

After the ordeal of her "test", Barbara was glad to be back at a computer screen, in the comparative peace of the office. The "lists" turned out to be a mass of complicated names and measures and Barbara forgot all about singing and nursing – even about Grandma Robinson; she thought of nothing other than transferring drugs and figures and making them balance. Her worries submerged in masses of facts and figures, her fingers tap-tapping on the keys, her head full of Latin names and complicated numbers, she lost all track of time… until a familiar voice caught her attention:

"Ah, Sister Tate – a word?"

Dr Craster came drifting into the office, smiling vaguely and looking ten years younger than he did on the ward. Then he saw Barbara and stopped short.

"Sister's out on the ward," she told him.

But he moved on into the office and glanced at the computer. "So – you're taking the opportunity to practise the new technology," he observed.

"No," she corrected him. "I'm bringing the drugs list up to date."

His bright blue eyes widened in surprise and disapproval, she noted with dismay.

"But surely that's an administrative task," he said.

"And we have no administrator today," she pointed out.

He sighed. "We're certainly the Cinderella department of this hospital," he said. "However, that's no reason why you should have admin. duties dumped on you."

"Oh, I'm very experienced in this so-called 'new technology'." She swivelled round and threw him a cool, amused glance. "It takes me half the time it takes anyone else on the ward and relieves Sister Tate for real nursing duties."

"But that's what you're here to learn – nursing, not administration, surely?"

"And surely the one backs up the other," Barbara argued. "Good administration is the foundation of good nursing."

He looked at her thoughtfully. "That's a very interesting theory," he observed. "But you should be out among the patients, not shut away in the office."

He sees it as a soft option, thinks I'm skiving off the ward, Barbara thought indignantly.

"Excuse me, Dr Craster," she said acidly. "I was under the impression that Sister Tate is in charge of my placement in geriatrics."

"And so she is," he assured her.

"She asked me to do this relatively minor

administrative task in my coffee-break, knowing I'm well qualified to do so." She stood up. "I'm just going back to the ward now," she said, "if you'll excuse me." She stood in front of him, waiting for him to move out of her way. He didn't.

" 'Shall we dance?' " he asked, his usually sombre expression cracking open in a broad grin.

And, to her surprise, Barbara found herself grinning back.

Things were quiet on the continuing care ward; Barbara assisted Mark with the personal care charts, smiling to herself as she wrote in the urine measures. "Good record-keeping means good nursing," she told herself, reminded of her recent encounter with "young" Dr Craster. Young only in the sense of an assistant consultant – he had to be thirty-something. But possibly young at heart? she wondered, remembering his grin.

"Happy in your work?" Mark asked sarcastically. This was one of everyone's least favourite routine tasks.

"Love it," she replied ironically, watching him tapping the urine from the patient's bag into a flask.

Suddenly the patient above spoke.

"Hello! Is that the singing nurse?"

Mark looked startled. "Nobody singing here, Harold," he said.

Barbara moved closer to the bed and was quite

shocked to see Mr Gough's bright, rather bulging eyes looking up at her. The last time she'd seen him was with Evie Wilde in the Day Room, erect and dapper in spite of his shaking and his stick. Now he looked small and shrivelled, his pyjama jacket bunched up around his scraggy neck as if it were four sizes too big and his head nod-nod-nodding continually. And he was occupying a continuing care bed, she observed, and that often meant one thing – no cure.

"Miss Wilde told me you were a singer," he said.

"Oh no, I'm a student nurse," Barbara assured him – or was she assuring herself? she wondered.

"She said she was going to sing a duet with you."

Barbara laughed. "Well, maybe one day – if she'll teach me one of her songs. Did you know she was a professional?"

The old man nodded. "Of course I did," he said. "Evie Wilde, the Salford Sweetheart – recognized her as soon as she arrived."

"You recognized her?"

He nod-nod-nodded and his mouth widened in a quivering smile. "Used to go to the Withington Empire every Saturday night. Top of the bill she was, in those days."

"Was she really? She must have been famous then."

"Mobbed at the stage door many a time." Mr Gough smiled at the recollection.

Just then, Mark stood up abruptly, swinging a urine bottle at his side.

"125 cc's," he announced.

Barbara looked down at her chart.

"We need to do the urinalysis tests," she said. "I'll see you again soon, Mr Gough – we're off to the prep room now."

"Come and sing to me some time, nurse," he said. "You and Evie together."

"I'll see what we can do," Barbara promised.

"What's all this singing business?" asked Mark as he put out the samples for the lab collection.

"Oh – you know Evie Wilde?"

"Do I not?" he winced. "Arrogant, rude and spoiled rotten!"

"Perhaps she is," said Barbara thoughtfully. "But I suppose when you've been a great star you find it difficult to be old and helpless."

"She's not helpless – has half the men in the Day Room bringing her cups of tea!"

"Charm," said Barbara. "She's still got the magic."

"Not for me, she hasn't," said Mark, lining up the sample tubes in order. "If she was that famous, why isn't she in a private nursing home instead of lording it over everybody here."

Barbara shrugged. "That was a long time ago," she said. "Evie Wilde won't have earned a penny in years – and probably never thought of saving any. She could be one of the poorest people in Tinsdale."

"She obviously doesn't think so. Treats the place like a hotel and us like its staff."

Barbara laughed. "Where have I heard that before?"

"From your mum, I'll bet."

"No, my grandma," Barbara said. "She says that when I'm home and rush off clubbing every night."

And suddenly she caught her breath, her eyes filled with tears, and she turned quickly away.

"Got the labels?" Mark asked, noticing nothing.

"Yeah," Barbara mumbled. She reached for a tissue from the rack and blew her nose hard. Stupid! she told herself. Ma had assured her only twelve hours ago that Grandma Robinson was quite all right. Shaking the tears away, she bent to check the label, peeled it off and handed it to Mark.

"Number five," she said. "G. Collins – X13/504."

"Number five it is," he agreed. "G. Collins – X13/504." He took the label and stuck it on the sample. "Next?"

"Number six, H.B. Gough – X28/397."

"Number six, H.B. Gough – X28/397."

Barbara watched him stick the label on to Mr Gough's sample. What would the test show up? she wondered. He had Parkinson's, she'd bet on it. He'd probably had it for years and now the drugs had stopped taking effect – it was a typical pattern. Poor

Mr Gough! she reflected. Such a pleasant, charming man...

But even as she thought about him, she was testing herself on his case. If it was Parkinson's disease, what was the treatment, the outcome, the nursing regime? Her mind busily worked out all the alternatives she could think of. There might be a question in the exams... Barbara reached for another label.

And all the time, at the back of her busy, professional thoughts, lay Grandma Robinson, rigid and still and unusually silent, in her hospital bed 150 miles away.

Chapter 6

"How's your grandma?"

Barbara was startled by the enquiry – especially as it came from Nikki Browne, who was rarely seen in Kelham's top-floor kitchen these days.

"Oh – well, ticking over, you know."

Nikki nodded. "Doesn't sound like the grandma we've heard about so long," she observed.

"No, I really don't think she is. I mean, according to my mother, there's no emergency or anything. They've done some tests and are 'awaiting results'."

"That's what they did with my dad last year," Katie joined in. "I was worried sick."

"Yes, of course. I remember." Barbara nodded. Katie's dad, her only relative, had been taken ill in their first term at St Ag's. It was only now that Barbara realized what she'd gone through. "You took it all very well," she told Katie.

"Well, actually, I was all right once I'd been over to see him. I mean, he looked pretty awful – all pale and feeble, but even so, to have seen for myself, talked to him – you know…"

"Yes, I'd feel a lot better if only I could see Grandma," Barbara said. "But it's so expensive – and it'd take at least a couple of days just when I've got so much work on."

"Well, once they'd done all the tests and got a diagnosis, Dad was better in no time. It'll probably be the same with your gran," Katie comforted her.

"Thanks, Katie – I hope you're right," said Barbara. And changing the painful subject, she turned to Nikki. "Haven't seen you in ages," she said. "How's the work going?"

Nikki groaned. "I'll never remember a thing for these exams," she said. "Some of my notes from term one read like a foreign language."

"Use Nick's," Katie advised. "I'll bet he's got them all typed up and filed in order."

"Of course he has!" said Nikki, a little bitterly.

Barbara looked at her. "Everything all right?" she asked.

Nikki sighed. "I suppose so," she said. "It's just that Nick's such a workaholic. Even after a day on Children's he comes back all ready to work –

seminars, voluntary lectures, revision, revision, revision – I can't keep up with him."

"That's Nick Bone for you," said Katie, shovelling sugar into her tea. "Determined to be student of the year, whatever the cost."

"Oh now, that's a bit unkind. I think he's just after making Nikki student of the year," smiled Claire.

"I'll never be that – don't even want to. A modest pass, that's all I ask." Nikki bent her head over her coffee mug, letting her fine, fair hair flop down so that her face was almost hidden. "But I'm so muddled I don't feel capable of even that right now."

"Seems to me you need a break," Barbara advised. "From work, from college – possibly even from Nick."

"Nick has a strong personality," Claire commented.

"And oodles of charm," grinned Katie, who had quite fancied Nick herself in their early days at St Ag's.

"Even so, you mustn't let him take you over like this," said Barbara. "Look – why don't you come over to the Medics' Mess this Friday evening? We haven't seen you there lately."

"Are you singing?" Nikki asked.

"Yes, but don't let that put you off," smiled Barbara.

Nikki smiled back. "It won't," she said. "But it might persuade Nick – you know how keen he is on your jazzy numbers."

"Well, there'll be plenty of those," Barbara assured her, "and some new stuff of Theo's too."

"And dancing to follow," Katie said. "Nick loves dancing." She closed her eyes and swayed to and fro as if remembering the previous summer, when she and Nick had danced together all night at the St Ag's Centenary Ball.

Claire nudged her – hard. "Katie!" she muttered. "You really are a tactless idiot."

"What? Oh – yes!" Katie clapped a hand over her mouth. "Sorry, Nikki – didn't mean…" She was really embarrassed, for Nikki was no dancer. On the rare occasions she'd come to college discos she'd always sat out, sipping a drink, enjoying the music but far too inhibited to get up and join in.

But now she smiled. "It's all right, Katie," she said. "Nick's been teaching me how to dance. I'm quite looking forward to demonstrating my talent."

"Great!" said Barbara. "It'll do you both good to relax."

"Yes, it will," said Nikki decisively. "Thanks, Barbara. It's a wonderful idea."

"Oh, she's full of them!" said Katie. "If you ever have a problem, Aunty Ba's got the answer!" She lifted her mug in a mock toast. "Here's to Aunty Ba!"

74

"And Friday night!" added Nikki, smiling happily.

First get through the day, thought Barbara, weaving her way through the ambulances parked outside Tinsdale on Friday morning. They were waiting to pick up "weekenders" – patients who went home when their families were around to take care of them. The atmosphere in the foyer was the very opposite of Mondays, Barbara suddenly realized: there was a jolly, festive air about, people propelled themselves around in their chairs or shuffled behind their zimmers, joking with each other and with the ambulance staff who shepherded them along.

"They're like children out on a treat," she observed to Sister Tate.

"Och aye," the Sister agreed. "It's the best medicine – knowing you're going home to someone you love."

That would certainly be the best medicine for Grandma Robinson, Barbara reflected. If only there were someone home to take care of her...

"You think old people should be kept at home as much as possible?" she asked.

"Well, of course," Sister Tate said. "Ageing is not an illness. They shouldn't be in an institution unless they are ill. Just like anyone of any age."

"But if there's no one at home to look after them?"

"Ah well, that's not a medical problem, is it? That's the responsibility of the Social Services – which reminds me, I have a heap of notes on my desk and a dozen phone calls to make." Sister Tate sighed. "I was going to spend some time in the Day Room – it always feels rather empty this time of the week. Depressing for those not going anywhere, you know?"

"It must be," said Barbara, thinking once more of her grandma, not going anywhere.

"So can you do the first round?" said Sister Tate. "Tea and sympathy – you know the routine well enough now."

As she entered the Day Room, Barbara had the feeling of gloom descending like rain clouds from the ceiling.

"Morning, everybody!" she said, loudly and cheerfully. "You all right this morning – Annie? Harry? How are you, Mabel?" She moved around, chatting to the residents but getting only a subdued response.

"And Miss Wilde – in good voice, are you?" She stopped at Evie Wilde's corner.

"I'm expecting a phone call," she said, as she always did at this time of day. "You'll have to take me to the office."

"No, it's all right, Miss Wilde; we have a telephone on a trolley – remember? I brought it to you yesterday."

"Yesterday?" Miss Wilde stared at Barbara. "I didn't get a telephone call yesterday."

"No, you didn't," Barbara agreed, wishing she'd never mentioned it. "We had a nice chat instead. You were telling me all about your brilliant career on the stage."

"Why?"

"Well, I'm a singer too – not famous or anything like you…"

"Ah! You're Barbara… Barbara … what's your other name?"

"Robinson. Student Nurse Robinson."

"Yes – and you sing."

Barbara nodded. "Yes, I sing," she agreed.

"Let me see you breathe," commanded Miss Wilde.

Barbara smiled; her years in the Gospel choir had taught her all about breathing. She stood up very straight, expanded her rib-cage, and let the air flow right down to the bottom of her lungs.

"Well done!" said her teacher. "Now, listen to this." And before Barbara could stop her, Miss Wilde embarked on a singing a scale, quietly, firmly and absolutely in tune. "Now – you," she commanded.

Barbara looked around. After all, she was supposed to be looking after the others too. But some were dozing, and the others gazed emptily at the huge television screen in the opposite corner.

Taking another deep breath, she sang the scale again.

"Mmmm – not bad. Need more head-tone, more projection, like this..."

And this time she sang a little louder, nodding to Barbara to follow her.

As the lesson continued Barbara was amazed how much she learned. By the time the tea-trolley arrived, she was singing single notes after Miss Wilde and already feeling more in control of her voice.

"We'll try the whole scale – ready?" Evie lifted up a thin white hand and they set off singing together.

"La, la, la, la, la, la, la, laaaaa!" At the end, Evie swept her elegant arm into the air and bowed her head slightly.

"Bravo!"

They both turned at the sound of applause from Dr Craster, who crossed the room bearing a cup of tea.

"Here you are, Miss Wilde – I think you've earned this."

"Oh, I don't know about that, young man," she smiled. "I think Nurse Robinson has been doing all the work."

"She's certainly been working hard at her *singing*," he agreed. And Barbara winced inwardly at the implication.

"I'll see how the others are getting on," she said, making a move.

But again, Dr Craster was in her way. "So – you're Mr Gough's singing nurse," he said, staring at her with his sharp blue eyes.

"Well, he does call me that," Barbara said, rather flustered. She didn't want him to think she went around singing at all the patients. "But he's really a fan of Evie's. Isn't he, Miss Wilde?" Quickly she turned back to the old lady.

"What? Speak up, gel! You'll never make a singer if your diction is poor."

"Harold Gough – he's your fan," Barbara said, very clearly.

"Oh, yes, he's a dear. Knows all the old theatres, all the old stars – all dead and gone long ago…" She sipped her tea thoughtfully. Suddenly she looked up, all alert. "Well, where is he? I haven't seen him in here for a day or two."

"No, he's not too well just now," Dr Craster told her. "We've given him a bed in the ward."

"That's a pity. He's the only interesting chap around here, you know," she told Barbara confidentially, quite ignoring the presence of Dr Craster.

Barbara suppressed a grin. One in the eye for "the young doctor", she thought.

"Would you like me to take you over to see Mr Gough?" she asked Miss Wilde.

"Oh, would you, darling? That is so kind." Evie Wilde flashed her brilliant, professional smile in Barbara's direction.

"I'll take you – I'm on my way to the ward." Dr Craster made a sudden move. "Come along, Miss Wilde – I'll help you into the wheelchair." He picked her up bodily and gently set her down in the wheelchair. "There you go!" he said.

"My goodness," she fluttered. "It's a long time since anyone did that!"

"Go on! I'll bet you have all the gentlemen at your feet."

"Well, there was a time, young man…"

And so, chatting together, charming each other, the doctor and Evie Wilde made their progress out of the Day Room.

Feeling as if she'd been dismissed, Barbara picked up Evie's unfinished tea and sipped it as she wandered off to chat with the other residents.

That man always seems to catch me at a disadvantage, she thought. Every time we meet I feel about twelve years old! Everybody else thinks I'm so sophisticated, so mature, but he turns me into a dithering young student – and he's the one who'll be contributing to my report! Well, I'd better find some way of demonstrating a few nursing skills, she decided.

Her opportunity came later in the day.

"I've got to dress Mrs Hall's leg ulcer," Mark told her. "Want to help?"

"Yes, please – I've never done one before," said Barbara. Ulceration was a big problem with elderly limbs. Even the slightest knock or wound could ulcerate, given sluggish circulation and poor diet; leg dressings were a regular part of geriatric nursing.

She collected the trolley and followed Mark up to the dressings room, where she was surprised to find Dr Craster in command. Doctors usually left such chores to the nurses.

"I'm not happy about this ulcer," he was telling Mrs Hall. "Is it hurting you?"

"No, doctor, not when I keep it up like this…"

He gently unwrapped the old dressing, chatting with the patient, explaining what he was doing – and why.

"There, you see? It's not getting much better now, is it?"

Dolefully, Mrs Hall had to agree, and Dr Craster went on talking to her, leading her up to the very delicate matter of an operation.

"If we could just put some fresh skin over it," he said, "that would encourage it to heal and all the new skin would grow."

"Shall I have to buy it?" she asked anxiously.

He smiled down at her. "Oh no," he reassured her. "You have to provide it." And he went on to tell her about the skin graft they were going to do. Barbara watched and listened, grudgingly admiring the way he took care to make Mrs Hall understand her treatment. His eyes sparkled, his face glowed, as if he were talking to some attractive young woman, not a fat old lady. He likes it! she suddenly thought. He loves his work. And the grudge left her – she'd always admired people who were enthusiastic about their work.

"...so, Monday morning, bright and early, we'll see you up in theatre," he said. "You'll have a nice little sleep and when you wake up your leg will be dressed and all set to mend. You'll have a bit of a sore patch on your thigh – nothing to worry about."

"Thank you, doctor. When can I go home?"

"If everything goes to plan, you should be going home by the end of the week. Not on your feet, though. You have someone to take care of you?"

"I have that, doctor. I have the most wonderful husband in the world." Mrs Hall smiled and nodded happily.

"And he's got a pretty wonderful wife, I'd guess," Dr Craster said solemnly. "You've been very brave. I'm only sorry nothing's worked so far. But this little operation should start it healing."

He patted her shoulder and nodded to Mark to do the dressing.

"Keep her talking," he muttered to Barbara. "Messy, painful business. Get her distracted."

So Barbara asked Mrs Hall all about her wonderful husband, and by the time she'd finished extolling his virtues, her leg was neatly bound up again.

"Thank goodness that's over!" Mark gave a sigh of relief as they pushed the dressings trolley back up the ward. "And thank you," he smiled up at Barbara. "You did a great job there – it's always easier if the patient is relaxed."

"My pleasure," Barbara smiled. "I think I'm better at chatting than dressing," she admitted. "I'm cranky-handed."

"Cranky-handed? What's that?"

"It's my grandma's phrase," Barbara smiled. "According to her all men are cranky-handed and all women – except for me – are minty-clean."

Mark laughed. "She has a way with words, then, your gran?"

And suddenly Barbara was struck by a pang of anxiety so strong she could only nod.

"Well, anyone can learn to do a neat dressing," Mark said, thinking she was worried about her lack of skill. "But not everyone can keep the patient so relaxed. You have the charm for it."

Charm – not a word Barbara had ever associated with nursing before. More show-biz, she thought to herself, and she was suddenly reminded of Evie Wilde and her fan. She excused herself to Mark and went down to the long-stay ward.

Approaching Mr Gough's bed she paused for a moment, and saw that he was sleeping. Miss Wilde, holding one of his ever-trembling hands in hers, was singing softly. Barbara drew closer and stood behind the wheelchair. She listened for a moment, then, humming softly, added a harmony to Miss Wilde's tune. For a few moments the two women watched over the sick old man, singing together softly.

"Thank you, ladies." Harold Gough opened his staring eyes and smiled up at them both. "My own private duet!" He sighed and settled down to sleep.

Evie Wilde extracted her hand from his, patted him lightly, and turned to look back at Barbara, tears in her eyes.

"Take me back now," she ordered. "I'm expecting a telephone call."

As she pushed the chair out of the ward, Barbara caught a glimpse of Doctor Craster and Sister Tate, in conference over the bed by the exit. Fleetingly she wondered whether he'd overheard the duet. Another wrong impression, she thought; well, this time she didn't care. Mr Gough was sleeping peacefully, Evie Wilde was still high from her performance, and her sudden anxiety about Grandma Robinson was quite soothed away.

There's one more natural therapy for you, Dr Craster, she smiled to herself – music. And there are worse things to be than a singing nurse!

Chapter 7

Feeling much more of a singer, in her high heels and slim, black dress, than a nurse, Barbara made her way over to the Medics' Mess early on Friday evening. She and Theo were hoping for a quiet rehearsal before the club opened. And maybe a quiet talk, she thought, clutching her nurse's cloak around her in the cool, damp wind. Theo was pushing hard for that recording session but she was determined to resist just then: they were not nearly good enough for that. Never likely to be unless they put in a lot more rehearsal, and they certainly couldn't do that with their current combined work load.

She click-clicked her way round the back of the Medics' Mess. Theo was supposed to have organized this early start but you never knew with him. She hammered hard on the kitchen door. To her surprise, it opened immediately.

"Steady on, Ba!" called Nick Bone. "Come to storm the place or merely tune up?"

"A bit of both, perhaps," she grinned.

"Well, Theo's hard at it – in the back room with some people."

"People?" Barbara grimaced. Neither Theo nor she welcomed an audience at rehearsals. They had little enough time together as it was.

"Yeah. I thought maybe you were expanding into a group?"

"No way!" Barbara frowned. Was this one of Theo's new developments? "Hey, you're early, aren't you?" she said, changing tack.

"I'm on bar duty tonight, so make sure you don't get the fans too excited."

"Oh, I thought Nikki was bringing you for an evening's relaxation?"

"She'll be along with the others, I expect," he said evasively. And now he, too, quickly changed the subject. "So, how's Grandma Robinson now?"

"A bit better, apparently," Barbara said. "Last time Mum rang she said she was sitting up and taking notice, but they're still doing tests and still waiting for results."

"That's a long time for diagnosis, isn't it?" Nick observed. "We'd never muck about like that at St Ag's."

"Well, that's London for you," Barbara shrugged, unwilling to admit her own uneasiness on the subject. "Everything's cut back to the bone – if you'll pardon the expression." She went across the kitchen area to the club-room door. "See you later, Nick," she said. "Enjoy!"

"Some chance!" he grinned. "But save a dance for me at the end of the evening."

He should be saving them all for Nikki, Barbara thought. But it was none of her business and she had quite enough to worry about without acting as "Aunty Ba" to those two!

As she crossed the dance floor she could hear Theo tinkling the piano keys in a room nearby. Humming his tune, she went over to join him – and his audience.

"Ba, this is Kent – and Josie. They're from the recording studio I told you about – you know, where we want to make our demo tape?"

"Where *you* want to make *your* demo tape," she reminded him. "Hi, Kent, Josie!"

She saw the girl had close-cropped hair, bleached white so that it was scarcely visible on her scalp, and a small, pinched face, with brightly painted lips – at that moment clamped around a long, tipped cigarette. Kent, in contrast, had hair flowing over his shoulders, dark and rippling, and a round, plump face, like a currant bun.

"Hello there, Ba," he said in a soft, wet voice.

Canadian, she thought, rather than American. Josie gave no indication that she'd seen her.

Theo said, "I thought we'd run through some of our standards, give them a sample of the sound, then maybe show them a few of mine – all right?"

She could tell he was nervous by the way he spoke, eagerly, anxiously, not at all the laconic manner he usually adopted.

"Right," she said. "Let's go!"

She didn't really care whether they were impressed or not; she just sang, enjoying the sound and responding to Theo's improvisations so that everything "came good", as Kenny would have it. Even Theo's new songs, which had hardly had an airing, sounded right just then.

"You have a nice sound there," said Kent, during a break in the music.

"Yes, we do, don't we?" said Barbara. "But I think if we go on any longer we'll spoil the performance. We're just nicely tuned up now."

"But Kent and Josie – they might want to hear some more," Theo protested.

"They'll hear some more if they stay a while at the club."

"We gotta get back." It was the first time Josie had spoken.

Barbara winced at her mid-Atlantic whine. "Well, I've had a very busy day. If I use any more voice now I won't make much of a job later on," she said. She picked up her cloak and slung it round her shoulders.

"But Ba, this is important," Theo protested.

"And so's our performance tonight," she pointed out. "We're booked in for that."

There was an awkward pause. Josie dragged at her third cigarette and gazed into the far distance. Barbara flapped a hand to keep the smoke away. Theo sat miserably at the piano.

"Yeah, well, we'd better get going," said Kent. "Thanks, Theo, Ba – nice hearing you."

"Oh, yes, er, thanks for coming. We'll be in touch, right?" Theo's glasses flashed like distress signals as he looked from Kent to Josie and back again. "See you – soon, I hope…"

With neither a word of farewell nor a backward glance, Josie stalked across the room. Kent shrugged his shoulders and shuffled off after her.

Barbara pulled her cloak around her and began to collect up Theo's music.

"What did you do that for?" he asked.

"Do what?"

"Oh, come on, Ba – you put them right off just when they were getting interested."

"If they were interested why didn't they stay?"

"Because they had somewhere else to go – they're very busy people."

"And we aren't?" Barbara took a deep breath. "I don't know what you've been doing today, but I've been watching an old man die, I've been lifting paralysed people, pushing wheelchairs, carrying bed-pans, mopping incontinents. I'll bet that Josie hasn't spent a day like that in her life!"

"Of course she hasn't," Theo said impatiently. "But she does run that sound studio – she's not exactly idle."

"Not exactly sensitive either," said Barbara, flapping the edge of her cloak, "chain-smoking in a small room like this." She went over and ostentatiously opened the door, wafting the smoke about as she moved.

"This isn't about smoking, is it?" Theo suddenly said. He stood up and turned to face her. "You don't want to make this tape, do you?"

Barbara sighed. "So far as I remember," she said, "we agreed to take on the Chuzzlewit job and leave the tape until we felt ready. Now I don't feel we're at all ready, yet you invite a couple of professionals in to hear us rehearse. For God's sake, Theo, you might have warned me."

"Yes, I'm sorry." He had the grace to look shame-faced. "I just didn't have time. They rang late this afternoon, said they were in the area, could they come and hear us. I thought they meant at the gig, but they were here when I arrived. I could hardly tell them to get lost until eight, now could I?"

"Yes, you could. That would have been the professional thing to do. We don't perform until we're ready — we've always agreed on that. Even for a little charity do we've always been well-rehearsed."

"But we were well-rehearsed — we were terrific just now."

"Yes, we were," she agreed. "But if we'd have gone on in this smoky, stuffy atmosphere, we'd have had nothing left to give later. Our booking for tonight is with the Medics' Mess, not the studio."

"But our future lies with that tape, not with the footling Medics' Mess," said Theo.

Barbara groaned. "Our future lies with the medical profession," she reminded him, "not with a little recording studio."

"Wellworn Records are not a little recording company," Theo said quietly. "They're the most successful in the North."

"So they don't need us — and we don't need them." Barbara turned to go into the club-room.

Theo followed. "But we do need them — if not now, then later on. They're our insurance," he said desperately. "If we make a go of Chuzzlewit's and want to branch out, they're the people for us."

Barbara sighed. "Look, Theo, if I've upset your plans I'm sorry. But they are *your* plans, not mine. All I want to do now is to get through this gig, through the final week of my placement and through my exams — with distinction. That's how I see my future, all right?"

Theo stood by the keyboard, looking up at her for a moment. "I think we're going to have to talk this over another time," he said.

"There's nothing to talk over – but all right, some other time. Now, let's just get tonight's programme sorted. Shall we start with one of yours?"

They went through their usual routine: Theo tinkling in the background as the club filled up, then, later, Barbara joined him and the crowd quietened down and settled back to listen seriously. This was the moment Barbara looked forward to, starting very quietly with a smoky, smoochy love song, sung as if to Theo, then a quick change to livelier numbers, following Theo's clever improvisations, teasing and laughing with him after an especially tricky section. Barbara always enjoyed the performance more than the applause at the end. But not tonight. Tonight the atmosphere was electric with their disagreement and she kept her distance from the keyboards, singing directly out at the audience rather than with Theo's accompaniment.

So they went into their final number without even having exchanged a glance. But the audience seemed to like it. They clapped and stamped and whistled and cat-called as they usually did, apparently unaware of the tensions on the platform. Barbara bowed slightly then extended an arm towards Theo, inviting him to come down and stand at her side to share the applause. But Theo didn't move; he stood by the keyboard and merely nodded curtly before leaving the platform. Barbara flashed a brilliant smile out to the audience and followed him, determined to have things out right there and then. They couldn't possibly start on a new gig in this mood.

But Theo had already gone.

Damn! she thought. He must have walked straight out of the back door – and he was on call at midnight. For a moment she thought of following him, but suddenly she simply didn't have the energy. She'd call him tomorrow. They'd sort it all out then, when she could think more clearly.

Slipping her cloak around her shoulders, she went round to join the Kelhamites in the club-room. The music was on tape now and several couples were already dancing. Barbara skirted the tiny dance floor and made her way over to the bar – she needed a drink after that performance.

But her way was blocked – again – by a tall, big man, propping up the bar just where she wanted to be served.

"Oh – Dr Craster! I haven't seen you here before."

"No, I don't often have the time, especially when Mr Coulthard is around." He didn't move. "Congratulations," he said. "That was quite some performance."

"Thank you," Barbara said.

"So what'll you have?"

"Thank you – Coke – lemon and ice, thanks."

He ordered her drink and a beer for himself, then leaned back on the bar and looked down on her. "Well, for what it's worth, SN Robinson, I think you're wasting your talent in Geriatrics."

Barbara frowned. Even if he meant that, it wasn't exactly flattering. After all, he would be filing a report on her performance in Geriatrics, not on the platform tonight.

"I don't have to settle for Geriatrics," she pointed out.

"But you're determined to settle for nursing?" he persisted.

Barbara sighed. Why couldn't everybody leave her alone to get on with her job – her real job? But what was that?

"I have another two years at least before I settle for anything," she edged.

"But enough talent to settle for show-biz right now, I'd say."

"With respect, Dr Craster, you're a geriatric consultant, not a theatrical agent."

"You're right!" he laughed – a big, echoing laugh that carried even over the music. "And I must admit, I'm biased."

"Biased?" she repeated, puzzled.

"As a member of your fan club," he said. "Do you sing here regularly?"

"Most Fridays," she hedged. Was he testing her out?

"It must take some rehearsing, keeping up a repertoire," he observed.

Meaning I neglect my college work? she wondered. "Oh, they're mostly standards," she said airily. "I've known them for years."

"Your drinks!" Nick put the glasses on the bar in front of them. "It was great, Ba!" he said, giving her a thumbs-up. "Where's Theo?"

Barbara blushed. "Oh – he's had to get back on call," she said.

"Ah, that explains it," said Nick. "He wasn't really with it, heart and soul, tonight – know what I mean?" He winked at her and went over to serve someone else, leaving Barbara feeling worse than ever.

"Cheers!" said Dr Craster.

Barbara picked up her glass and took a long drink of the ice-cold Coke. "Cheers," she said dolefully.

"He's right, you know," Dr Craster said, indicating Nick. "I'd have thought your voice could stand up to a heavier backing than keyboards."

"Well, I do sing with my brother's band at home," she said. "But of course, that's quite a different sound – rock, you know, heavy stuff."

"I can imagine your voice rising to a challenge like that," Dr Craster said. "You should find yourself a really good backing group, make a demo. I've an old school friend in the music business might help…"

For a moment Barbara stared at him. *Get thee behind me…* she thought. She tipped up her glass and drained it.

"I must go," she said. "Thanks for the drink."

"Oh, you can't do that," he protested. He stood towering over her, blocking her way – again.

"Shall we dance?" he grinned.

Barbara wondered whether to give him the push – literally – or to accept. As she hesitated, he slipped her cloak off her shoulders, draped it over a stool, and led her on to the dance floor.

"I'm Mel," he said, close to her ear. "Do you come here often?"

And so they danced – not one, but several dances. Barbara was aware of Katie's curious eyes as they passed on the dance-floor at one point, aware, too, of Mel's blissful height towering over her, and his surprising grace as they gyrated together. She liked the way he danced seriously; most blokes just joggled around hopefully, leaving all the fancy work to their partner, but Mel really danced *with* her. Suddenly her worries about Theo, about work, about Grandma Robinson, all fell away. She laughed, she smiled, she sparkled – and Mel, she knew, was very impressed.

After a while they made their way back to the bar.

"I must get a drink," he said. "Haven't danced

like that since I qualified."

"Really?" she said. "Then it's time you relaxed a bit. What'll you have?"

"Iced tonic water," he said. "I'm driving."

"Right. Nick?" she called. She liked the way Mel accepted her offer of a drink without all that silly protesting some men put up. This was some nice guy, she thought, watching him mopping his now wild red hair and his very pink face. He caught her eye and for a second he looked right at her, direct and hard. Then Barbara looked away.

"Nick! Drinks please, love!" she called.

Nick came over, carrying the phone – and looking serious.

"Ba, Sister Thomas wants to speak to you," he said.

"To me?" Barbara wasn't worried. She was quite a favourite with Ann Thomas, she knew, and very much her right-hand woman when it came to running things at Kelham's. "Oh Lord! I hope there hasn't been a break-in or anything," she said lightly to Nick. He merely held out the phone to her without replying.

"Hello, Sister Thomas," Barbara said. "Something wrong at Kelham's?"

At first she couldn't make out what Sister Thomas was saying. She pressed her finger into her other ear, to shut out the noise at the bar.

"I didn't get that," she said. "So much noise…"

"I think you should come over to my flat – there's a message from home."

From home! Of course it would be. Only something as serious as that would have caused Ann Thomas to call her on a Friday night.

Barbara swallowed hard. "I'll be right over," she said, putting down the phone and staring blankly at Nick.

"Bad news?" he asked quietly.

"I don't know – yet."

And for a moment the music seemed to fade, the dancers receded into the distance, sweat dripped off her head and trickled down her back, her heart-beat seemed quite audible. She clutched at the bar.

Mel Craster gripped her arm.

"Here, sit down," he said, pushing her on to a stool.

"No – I must go!" She grabbed her cloak and turned to leave, pushing her way across the crowded floor, through the crashing music which only a moment ago had sounded so sweet.

"Hang on!" Mel called. "I'll drive you over."

But she couldn't stop. She had to keep on moving, unthinking, unfeeling, unseeing, just moving...

He caught up with her at the exit.

"You can't walk alone across the grounds at night," he told her. "Come on – my car's at the front."

He didn't ask her anything, just packed her into

the car, drove in silence over to Kelham House and pulled up at the door.

"Thanks for the lift." She opened her door but he stopped her and pushed a card into her hand.

"If there's anything I can do – anything – just ring," he said.

"Yes – thank you," she replied, gripping the card as if it were a life-line. Without turning to wave, she walked up the steps, unlocked the door and went quickly into Kelham's.

Chapter 8

Rob – of all people – met her at Euston. Barbara dropped her bag and held out her arms to him, quite forgetting how much he disliked being hugged. For a moment he buried his head in her shoulder and they both wept a little.

He stood back. "You look terrible," he grinned.

"You surprised?" she sniffed. "Last night was just a waste – a waste!" she repeated bitterly, remembering the hours she'd lain weeping. Of course Sister Thomas had been very kind, letting her use her telephone to talk to Ma, plying her with hot drinks and a sleeping pill, but even she couldn't conjure up transport at that time of night. "Would you believe? No trains after nine, no coaches after eight – I felt so helpless, not getting here sooner."

"Well, you weren't the only one," he reassured

her. "I was in the studio sorting my late-night programme, Kenny was doing a gig in some college out west, Dad can't get on a flight until tomorrow..."

"Poor Ma," said Barbara. "All on her own."

"Except for half-a-dozen aunties, a smattering of uncles, all the cousins and half the Adventists in London," said Rob drily.

"It's not the same," Barbara insisted. "It's us she needs and we weren't even here with Grandma when ... when she died."

"Nobody was," said Rob, "so don't go blaming yourself." He picked up her bag. "Come on," he said. "I've borrowed Mum's car – and her *Nurse Calling* badge. We're on double yellows."

Barbara strode after him. "What do you mean, 'nobody was'?" she demanded.

"You can get all the details at home – come on!"

Rob was right: the little flat was overflowing with friends and relatives, flowers and food, and, no doubt, thought Barbara, sniffing the air, bottles and cigarettes as well.

"Mum!" She took her mother into her arms, and for a moment they clung together in the little hall, weeping quietly, just holding on. Eventually, her mother broke away.

"My cardigan's quite wet through," she laughed nervously. "Come on in now, get yourself somethin' – you must be starved!"

She sounds just like Grandma, thought Barbara – and the tears started again.

It was a long time before the house calmed down. All day people trooped through: market traders, church members, old ladies, Sunday School children, the Asian family from the paper shop, the Chinese from Grandma's favourite restaurant – all bringing condolences and gifts. Barbara had never realized how important Grandma Robinson had been to so many people.

"Where on earth did she meet all these people?" she whispered to Kenny.

"Had a busy life, our gran," he said. "Lots of folk fond of her."

"Obviously," said Barbara, wishing they'd all go away. Her face ached with smiling, her eyes were sore with tears, her head spinning with exhaustion. All she wanted to do was to crawl into her bed, pull the quilt over and shut them all out for at least a few hours. Her brothers, however, had other ideas.

"Can you take over?" Rob asked. "I've got a meeting at the station in an hour – next week's schedules, you know?"

"The show must go on?" Barbara mocked.

"Yeah, that's right," Rob said. He looked straight at her. "And Grandma Robinson would be the first to agree with me. See ya!"

He went over to kiss their mother and whisper something to her. She nodded, smiled, and waved him away.

Kenny was next.

"Look, I've got a gig at the Cellar tonight," he told Barbara. "If I cancel it leaves the boys in a hell of a mess…"

"Well, you go and do it – if you can face it," she said. "After all, that's what Rob's done."

Kenny hesitated. "He's right though, Ba," he said. "Grandma Robinson was always one for keeping the work going."

"Grandma Robinson didn't even recognize what you and Rob do as work," Barbara shot back.

"Men's work," Kenny grinned. "Not important like having babies and making chilli pickles."

And Barbara couldn't help smiling back at him.

"Go on, then," she said. "I'll take care of Ma tonight."

"Thanks, doll – I'll take over tomorrow," Kenny promised.

Tomorrow, thought Barbara. There must be a thousand things to do before tomorrow.

"What about the funeral – who's arranging all that?" she asked Kenny.

He shrugged. "Dad, I suppose, when he gets here."

And Barbara suddenly realized that it would all be up to her father. Grandma Robinson was, after all, his mother. Barbara looked across the room, to where her own mother was holding court, nodding patiently, smiling away the tears, listening to some old man's memories of her mother-in-law. But behind the twinkling glasses the eyes were blank, and her face had paled to a dusty grey. Barbara decided it was time for action.

Half an hour later the house was quiet, her mother was stretched out on the sofa, half-dozing, and Barbara was in the kitchen defrosting a pan of pumpkin soup — made, she suddenly realized, by Grandma Robinson.

"I don' waste no pumpkin on hallowe'en lanterns," she'd said indignantly, when Kenny had tried to beg one for a gig. "I makin' spicy soup ready for the wintah."

Now Barbara had opened up the last carton. Tears dripped off her nose and into the soup; she sniffed, hoping Grandma Robinson had been scant with the salt, then smiling through the tears as she remembered Grandma's motto when cooking: "Can always add salt after you cooked — can't ever take none away!"

Well, she was adding some then — just for you, Gran, she said inwardly, sniffing away the tears and pouring the rich golden liquid into two bowls.

She placed the tray on the coffee table.

"Come on, Ma!" she said, falsely cheerful. "Now they've all gone we can eat in peace."

Her mother sat up.

"I'm not that hungry," she said.

"I know," Barbara agreed. "But we'll both feel better if we eat. Comfort food, remember?"

And her mother picked up her spoon, smiling.

"Yes – a great one for comfort food, your grandmother," she said. Then, "I shall miss her, you know."

"I know you will – we all will."

They sipped their soup for a while in silence. Then, seeing her mother relax, her colour improve, Barbara spoke.

"Want to tell me how it happened?"

Her mother looked surprised. "Didn't Rob explain?" she asked.

"When did he ever?"

"Well," Selina Robinson sighed, "I called in to see her on my way down to Maternity. She was sitting up, had a cup of tea, felt very tired, she said – that's all she complained of all week." She paused to mop her eyes. "That and wanting to come home," she added. "I was trying to juggle schedules and bring her back here, if only for the weekend, but you know what Maternity's like this time of year."

"I do!" said Barbara. "Grandma calls them 'holiday babies'!" She paused, then added, "*Called* them, I mean."

"Yeah," her mother smiled sadly. "Nine months after the summer in the sun – they're popping up all over the place this week. It's funny, you know –

I eventually got Bev to agree to double up on Sunday and I was so pleased that as soon as I had a free moment I rushed back to tell Emmelia she was coming home ... and that's when I found her..."

Barbara swallowed hard. "Dead?" she asked.

"Oh yes. I knew that straight away."

"Oh, Ma, it must have been terrible for you!" Barbara leaned over and gently touched her mother's shoulder. "Why on earth didn't they ring to get you?"

"Well, that was the really horrible part – nobody knew she'd gone."

"What do you mean?" Barbara was puzzled: even she, a mere first-year student, could tell the difference between a live patient and a dead one.

"Well, you know how it is with staffing these days. They thought I was with her, had an emergency on another section – she just slipped away when nobody was around."

"Oh, Ma!" Barbara wailed aloud at the thought of Grandma Robinson, gregarious, extrovert, never alone for more than an hour or two in her waking life, dying completely alone.

"Hush, darlin'!" Her mother took her hand and held it tight. "We're all on our own when we die," she said. "Nobody can go with us."

Silence. Both women thought about Emmelia Robinson, all alone, slipping quietly away – no drama, no final farewells, no trouble to anyone, just as she'd lived.

Barbara stirred. "When can I see her, Ma?"

Her mother shook her head doubtfully. "They'll have taken her down to the mortuary by now."

"What for?" Barbara was shocked. On the train home, she'd imagined herself in the chapel of rest, at the funeral parlour down the road, sitting quietly with Grandma Robinson, all cleansed and neat in a lace-lined coffin, soft music playing…

"Autopsy," said her mother briefly.

Of course! She ought to have known. If the medical profession didn't know what was making Grandma Robinson ill, they certainly wouldn't know what killed her.

"Best wait until the funeral," her mother advised.

"When will that be?"

Selina Robinson shrugged. "It's up to your pa," she said. "We can't make any arrangements until after the autopsy." She thought for a moment. "I hope he'll make it Friday afternoon, then you can get back here easily."

"Back – what do you mean? I'm not going off up to Brassington leaving you to cope with everything on your own."

"I shan't be on my own," her mother said. "Kenny's here for the next few days, Rob's taking care of your father, and you know what my family's like…"

"But Grandma Robinson would have wanted me to stay here," Barbara objected.

"Grandma Robinson would have wanted you to finish your placement with your usual high grade – you won't get that if you're sitting moping down here."

Barbara glared in sullen silence.

"Look, Barbie," her mother pleaded, "you're holding the fort right now while the boys do their work. Let them take over while you do yours – do them both good to take a bit of responsibility."

"And what about you?"

"Oh, holiday babies or no holiday babies, I've taken a week's leave."

"Seems to me we're all getting on with our own lives with never a backward glance for Grandma Robinson," said Barbara sullenly.

"She wasn't one for glancing backward," smiled her mother. "And we'll never forget her, now will we?"

They sat in silence for a few minutes. Then Selina yawned.

"'Lordy, Lordy, but I'm a-weary'," she said, quoting one of her Gospel songs.

Barbara stood up.

"Come on – off to bed with you. I'll clear up here."

And to her surprise, her mother didn't even protest. She stood and looked up at her.

"Thank you, darlin,'" she said. "You're a good girl. Emmelia was so proud of you."

Barbara hugged her mother close.

"Oh, Ma," she said, her voice cracking. "We should have been with her."

"No. We were all doing what she would have wanted us to do – working."

"I wasn't," Barbara admitted. "I was doing just what she didn't want me to do – singing."

"Oh, she was proud of your singing too, provided it was in chapel or earning your way through college. She just didn't want you to get side-tracked again, that's all." She looked sharply at her daughter. "Not thinking of taking up a music career, are you?"

Barbara shook her head. "All I'm thinking about right now is getting through next week," she said truthfully. "Are you sure you want me to go back to St Ag's?"

"Quite sure," said her mother. "You got a return ticket?"

Barbara shook her head. "Only a day return," she said. "It was cheaper than a single and I couldn't afford a full return."

"Never you mind – this is no time for economies. You take the train back up there – it's more comfortable than the coach. I'll pay for your ticket."

"Thanks, Ma. If that's what you want, that's what I'll do."

*   *   *

And it was what she wanted to do, Barbara realized, as she sat by the window watching the passing cars. There was nothing she could do in Brixton now, and so much she had to do in Brassington…

Suddenly she remembered her row with Theo – Lord, was it only last night? And he'd be wanting a rehearsal on Sunday afternoon and she'd no idea how to find him. Theo might well be on duty, or back in his flat, with his parents… She rushed to the phone and rang Kelham's.

Luckily Katie answered. Of all the Six, she was the one to appreciate the importance of a rehearsal.

"Look, can you get hold of Theo?" Barbara asked her. "Tell him I'll be back late Sunday evening and I'll get in touch about Wednesday."

"Wednesday?"

"Yeah – we have a gig in town."

"And you're going to do it?" Katie asked.

"I – I don't know. I'll have to talk to him about it."

"So you're coming back tomorrow night?"

"Yes. It's our final week on placement – you know how important that is."

"True, but what about – you know – the funeral?"

"We can't go ahead yet – autopsy."

"Oh Ba! We're all so sorry. Jan says especially to give his love to your mother. Would it be all right if he rang her?"

"Oh, I'm sure she'd be delighted to hear from Jan." Selina Robinson had driven Jan all the way back to his family in central Europe only months ago and they'd struck up a deep friendship then.

"We've all sent cards to you both," Katie went on, "but now you'll be back before they arrive."

"That was kind." Barbara swallowed hard. "I'll tell Ma to open them," she said. "See you tomorrow!"

"What time's your train – or is it coach?"

"Oh, train – no time for economies, Ma says. It arrives at 8.45 – I'll be in Kelham's by 9.30, with luck."

"Even sooner with a lift. Leave it to me, somebody will be there to meet you."

It would be Nick, Barbara decided, as the train pressed on northwards. He was always happy to give anyone a lift in his pride and joy – the red Celica. And suddenly she thought of Mel Craster – was it only Friday evening when he'd driven her back to Kelham's? Heavens! it seemed months ago. He'd been very tactful, very kind, she thought now, getting her back quickly without asking any intrusive questions. Suddenly she remembered the card he'd thrust at her – what had she done with it? Well, what did it matter? she asked herself: she was hardly likely to be ringing him anyway.

She sighed, thinking back to Friday evening when she'd been busy upsetting Theo, singing his songs, dancing with Mel Craster with never even a thought of Grandma Robinson. And she had died all alone, at just about the time of Barbara's final song, so far as Ma could tell.

Barbara reached for her handkerchief to mop up the tears, but they never really started this time. Many of her worries were over now, she suddenly realized. No point worrying about Grandma's test results – whatever they showed they wouldn't bring her back. And no point making a demo tape with Theo, or even singing at Chuzzlewit's, she suddenly realized. That girl Josie would find a singer for Theo's gig – maybe someone who'd be glad to make a demo tape. But not Barbara Robinson – she knew that now. From now on, she'd sing for pleasure, for fun, for charity – Katie was always fund-raising for something – but that was all. Now, she knew, it was all settled – she'd never turn professional.

"Not a singing nurse, Grandma," she whispered. "A well-qualified nurse who, just occasionally, sings."

And this time tears did spring into her eyes but she didn't mind. She dabbed her face and gazed stoically out through the darkness.

"Gird them there loins, Barbie-gal!" She could hear Grandma Robinson's voice in her mind. "Gal's gotta be ready do her best work Monday mornin'."

Chapter 9

Everyone seemed to want to do their best work Monday morning – four of the Kelham Six actually sat down to breakfast in what Katie called "Kelham's Korner" in the cafeteria. Nikki Browne and Jan were not on placement just then – they'd have a more leisurely start to the day, as Katie enviously pointed out.

"Oh, I don't mind," said Nick. "I've enjoyed my time on Children's – want to make the most of it this week."

"And I've got to be in Orthopaedics bright and early," groaned Claire. "You remember Mr Lester-Ellis, Katie?"

"Do I!" Katie pulled a wry face; she'd made quite an impression on the Head of Orthopaedics in her first few weeks at St Ag's – and not always a good one.

"Well, he's coming in today – wants to talk to me."

"There's a treat for you," grinned Katie. "It's more than he ever did to me when I was on Orthopaedics."

"I guess he's going to ask you to make it your special study next year," said Barbara.

"We'll all have to be deciding that soon," Nick pointed out. "Anyone got any ideas?"

"Oh yes," said Claire. "I'd like to do Theatre."

"Ugh!" Katie shuddered. "Give me real live patients every time." She glanced at her watch. "And I won't have any of those out on Community if I don't get going. 'Bye, you lot – see you tonight!"

She paused by Barbara's chair, leaned down and gave her a quick kiss on her close-cropped head.

"Hope it's not too hard on you, pet," she said. And was gone.

Barbara smiled round at her friends. Ma had been right, she thought; this was the right place to be, with friends to cheer you along and work to be done. Nick had collected her from the train last night and brought her back to a royal welcome in the kitchen at Kelham's – "Grandma Robinson's wake," Claire had called it. They'd sat round the table remembering the old stories Barbara had told them about Grandma, drinking fruit punch – made to Grandma's recipe, so far as Jan could remember it, and eating not-quite-Grandma's cookies. Barbara had been both touched and soothed by their gesture, and so thoroughly relaxed she'd actually slept right up until her alarm woke her.

Now she stood up to leave the breakfast table. "Mustn't be late – Monday's arrivals day on Tinsdale," she explained. "See you all tonight!" She looked round the table for a moment. "And, by the way – thanks, you lot, for everything. Know what I mean?"

And she left without looking back.

"Ach, I didn't expect you in today, Barbara," said Sister Tate, frowning up from her computer. "I thought you'd be in London all week."

Sister Thomas had obviously passed the word round, thought Barbara. She explained about the delayed funeral – and her intention of working through her final week on Tinsdale.

"Though I might have to go back on Friday," she said.

"Of course – you can leave whenever you need, Barbara, you know that. I'm very impressed with your sense of duty – you could have claimed compassionate leave. I'd still have given you 'highly recommended' on your report."

"Thank you, Sister Tate." Barbara felt a surge of rather sad pleasure at the thought of Grandma Robinson's reaction to that news. "But there are so many people I want to see here in Tinsdale, before I go back to college."

"Ah yes, that reminds me – Dr Craster was asking after you earlier on. He seemed to know you'd been called away…" Sister Tate smiled rather too knowingly for Barbara's comfort.

"I was really thinking of the patients," she said rather primly. "How's Evie Wilde getting on?"

Sister Tate groaned.

"Ach, we're having a bit of trouble with that one," she said. "Insists it's time she went home, but we can't get in touch with her housekeeper."

"You mean she's not come back from Spain?"

"If indeed she ever went," said Sister Tate grimly. "People try all sorts of tricks, you know, to get old folk into a home."

"But we're a hospital, not an old people's home."

"Exactly!" Sister Tate peered hopefully at her screen. "And if you can persuade Miss Wilde of the difference, you're a better nurse than I am!"

"I'll have a chat with her," said Barbara. She glanced over Sister Tate's shoulder. "Press *Return*," she said as she turned to leave.

"What? Oh – of course – thanks, Barbara! You're a pal!"

Barbara smiled to herself as she made her way over to the Day Room. Well, Sister Tate obviously thought she was the tops – but would Miss Wilde agree?

Evie Wilde was fuming.

"It's not good enough," she told a passing auxiliary. "They're keeping me prisoner here, you know. I can perfectly well go home, but they won't take me. I shall have to make a telephone call – bring me that gadget."

"Later, love," the auxiliary told her, rolling her eyes in Barbara's direction and tapping the side of her head. "Quite confused this morning," she muttered.

"Don't you believe it," said Barbara. "Good morning, Evie!" she greeted the old lady. "Sung any good songs lately?"

Miss Wilde's mutinous expression softened.

"Oh – it's that singing nurse," she said. "When are we going to have our little concert?"

"Later in the week," Barbara said, crossing her fingers. "But we'll have to practise our songs first."

"Of course, my dear. Where's the rehearsal schedule?" She looked around vaguely.

"Well, as there's just the two of us, I think we can make our own schedule, don't you?"

"But I'm going home later on – you'll have to come over to me to rehearse."

"Ah, well, that's what I wanted to see you about," said Barbara. "You see, if we're going to perform really well, we'll need to rehearse every day."

Miss Wilde nodded happily. "Yes, that seems reasonable," she said. "I'm sure *you'll* need a great deal of rehearsal."

"Oh, I shall," Barbara assured her. "And several lessons as well. So you see," she went on, "it'd be much easier if you stay on here this week. As we're both in the same department we can rehearse any time." She crouched down on her haunches and smiled up at Miss Wilde.

There was a pause. Evie Wilde looked back at Barbara, her eyes bright and knowing.

"So that's your ploy to keep me here," she said. "Well, it won't do. I have to get home – there will be telephone calls, letters—"

"And lessons and rehearsals here at St Ag's," Barbara pointed out. She got up, towering over Miss Wilde's chair. "Think about it," she said. "I've got to get on with my work now."

At the door she glanced back and saw that Evie Wilde was frowning and muttering over a little red notebook with a slim gold pencil, its red tassel bobbing and joggling as she wrote.

Making the rehearsal schedule, Barbara thought. Well, it was better than pining for home. Now all she had to do was to persuade Sister Tate to arrange a musical afternoon – what Evie Wilde would probably call a "*soirée*"!

"Student Nurse Robinson! I thought you'd been called home."

Barbara turned to see Mel Craster by the sluice-room door.

"I was. I came back last night," she said.

"I see," he looked around. "Well – have you a moment?"

He stood back to allow her to enter the cold, white-tiled room, where water gushed intermittently through the stainless steel sluices. Just the place for an assignation, Barbara told herself ironically.

"Look – are you sure you can cope?" he asked, looking really concerned. "I mean, geriatric nursing's not a lot of fun at any time, but when you've just lost an elderly relative..."

Barbara smiled at the thought of Grandma Robinson's reaction to that description.

"She'd have wanted me to finish the placement," she assured him.

He nodded. "The right sense of priorities," he commented.

"Well, she was a nurse herself. She knows – she knew – all about priorities. Like *patients first*."

"Oh – if only some of our managers believed that," he said. "Did you know they want to close down our long-care wards?"

"Close them down? But why?"

He shrugged. "Rationalization, they call it," he said. "We have sick patients, they have departments providing treatment – put the two together and you have a neat little pattern and save a great deal of money."

"But our long-stay patients don't have just one illness," Barbara pointed out. "I mean, where would you send Mr Gough? Neurology for his Parkinson's, Orthopaedics for a new hip, Ophthalmics for his cataract – and then there's Urology…"

"Exactly." He smiled at her. "Like to come and put that argument to the Management Committees this afternoon?"

"I'm sure you can do that very well on your own."

"I'd rather have you with me," he said softly.

Barbara regarded him seriously for a moment.

"You know that's not on," she said. "But for what it's worth, I'll tell you how my gran came to die, all alone, in the far reaches of an almost empty general ward…"

So she explained about the delayed tests, the delayed results, the poor staffing ratio, the lack of anyone with geriatric experience…

"I mean, at least on our long-stay wards we have enough staff to keep a check on patients. I don't think they're left alone more than half an hour at a time…" Barbara felt her eyes fill with tears – not of sadness now, but a burning indignation that Grandma Robinson had been left for hours unattended, untended. And now, it seemed, people like Harold Gough would undoubtedly share the same fate. General wards were busy places – patients often had to demand attention constantly and frequently before they were answered; Mr Gough would never do that – he'd lie there quietly alone.

She blinked away the tears and felt Dr Craster's hand on her arm.

"I do wish you could come to that meeting," he said. "They ought to hear someone who can speak from experience of both sides – 'provider' and 'consumer', as they would put it." He gripped her arm tightly. "Well, with your permission, I'll use your very moving example. I only hope I can make it half as effective as you've just done."

"Feel free," smiled Barbara. "Grandma Robinson would be happy to be in the midst of battle again."

He loosed her arm and she turned to go.

"Wait – can I ask you…?"

"What?"

"After it's all over – the funeral and all – and you're back in college – well, would you come out for a meal with me?"

Barbara looked at him thoughtfully.

"I mean – I don't want to intrude…" he was saying.

"Intrude?"

"Well – your pianist – Theo, isn't he…?"

Barbara laughed. "Oh, that's just a working partnership," she assured him. "Or at least it was…"

"Was?"

Barbara sighed. "A long story," she said. "I'll tell you another time."

"Like at dinner?"

She nodded. "At dinner," she agreed. "Ring me some time next week."

And somehow it made all the difference, knowing that once she got through the week, and, more importantly, through the weekend, there was a treat awaiting her: an interesting evening with an interesting man. Barbara went off to look for Sister Tate, feeling almost light-hearted.

"A concert?" Sister Tate almost squealed. "But you surely can't think of performing this week?"

"Well, I won't be here next," Barbara pointed out. "I just wondered if we keep it very casual – a sing-song with the others joining in, just to pass an afternoon along…"

"It's a great idea," Sister Tate agreed. "We used to have a special event every afternoon – music, exercise sessions, demonstrations – all kinds of things, until the cuts."

"Well, this won't cost a penny, so long as you allow Evie Wilde and me to rehearse now and then – lunch-times and after duty…"

"Rehearse away, dearie," Sister Tate beamed. "Anything to keep that woman off the subject of going home until I can get Social Services mobilized."

It wasn't until Evie Wilde pointed out their need for an accompanist that Barbara's sense of triumph waned.

"We can use yours," the old lady said, ticking off a little note with her tiny pen. "Now, we'll need to rehearse with him – this afternoon would be convenient."

"That'll be difficult," said Barbara. "He's a houseman – they barely get to sleep, never mind have any free time."

"That's all right," said Miss Wilde briskly. "You can give him our programme – I'm sure he's experienced enough to fill in. Meantime, we'll manage on our own."

She was right, of course, Barbara reflected. Theo was the obvious answer. Given notice, he could probably arrange to come over to Tinsdale for an hour some time in the week.

"I'll talk to him," she said heavily.

And she realized that was exactly what she'd promised Theo – to talk things over. Well, they had plenty to talk about now, she thought. But how on earth could she ask Theo to do her a favour when she was about to ruin all his carefully-laid musical plans?

Chapter 10

M en's Surgical lay in the oldest part of the hospital building – and right in the heart of the nineteenth century, thought Barbara, as she passed under the highly decorative iron girders which held up the arched corridor roof like so many tree trunks. Fat white radiators squatted under high, leaded windows topped with stained-glass panels – more like a church than a place of healing. Barbara reflected that Grandma Robinson would have approved of the combination – she always said good nursing was a mixture of science and faith, bless her. She smiled sadly to herself and walked on to the end of the corridor into the surgical unit.

"Is Dr Britner on?" she asked a passing Junior, who eyed her suspiciously.

"Technically," said the girl, "but you can never be quite sure with Theo. Can I give him a message?" This was obviously intended as a dismissal.

But having come so far Barbara was not prepared to be bullied by a mere Junior.

"Thanks, but I need to talk to him myself," she said, drawing herself up to her not inconsiderable height.

The Junior opened her eyes wide, obviously thinking she was in on a lovers' tiff. "You'd better have a look around then."

"I will – thank you," said Barbara coolly.

She stood at the entrance to the old-style Nightingale ward with about twenty beds either side, most of which had one or two visitors by them but no sign of any doctors.

At the other end of the long ward, Barbara knew there would be a Day Room meant for patients, but often taken over by staff now that even surgical cases were sent home so quickly. She set off to walk the length of the room, hoping she wouldn't encounter the Sister or Charge-nurse.

Many of the patients were quite seriously ill, all of them recovering from major surgery, and yet as Barbara passed their beds, every one of them looked up, smiled or nodded, half-whistled or waved – acknowledging her presence in a variety of reactions. Barbara didn't react – she was too intent on finding Theo. She paused at the entrance to the Day

Room, conscious of a distinct tang of tobacco in the air: somebody had been taking a quick smoke in there, strictly against hospital rules.

"Hello – it's Theo's little song-bird!" A white-coated, dark-skinned young man looked up from the depths of an armchair by the door. "Hey – great show on Friday!"

"Thank you." Barbara's tone was cold. She objected to being described as Theo's anything, but the songbird was too much. "Can you tell me where Theo is?"

"Can anyone ever!" The medic grinned and looked at his watch. "Well, he's been on all day – might have gone for a kip."

"Gone home, you mean?" Barbara's heart sank.

"No, back to the duty room – on the main corridor immediately before the entrance to the ward."

"Right. Thanks for the help."

"No problem. If you find him, remind him he owes me one tonight."

"Tonight?"

He nodded. "Yeah – I did his afternoon shift yesterday."

Barbara retraced her steps along the ward. Conscious now of the appreciative glances which followed her, she smiled graciously all round.

Theo obviously had something important on yesterday afternoon, she thought. You didn't swap a quiet Sunday afternoon shift for Monday post-op night unless it was urgent. And he certainly hadn't been rehearsing with her then. So what was he doing? she wondered as she knocked on the door marked "Duty Staff".

But nobody answered. She knocked again, this time much harder and longer. People passing in the corridor looked at her curiously so she didn't dare call out. Eventually she turned the door handle, which immediately yielded. The door opened and she found herself in a tiny cabin-like room with narrow beds on either wall and little else. On one of the beds, still clad in a crumpled white coat, his hair a tangled mass on the thin pillow, lay Theo, deep in sleep.

Barbara hesitated: she knew enough about a houseman's working hours to appreciate Theo's need for sleep. On the other hand they just had to get things straightened out before Wednesday. She looked around for something on which to write a message, and as she moved Theo stirred, yawned and opened his eyes.

"Hello, Theo – I was trying not to disturb you," she said quietly.

"Well, you didn't succeed," he muttered grumpily.

"Oh, I'm sorry – look, you go back to sleep. Just ring me later, will you? We've got to talk."

"Barbara!" Thoroughly wakened now, Theo sat

up. "What are you doing here? I thought you were in London – your grandma…"

"Yeah," Barbara nodded, sighed, and told the whole story again. "So you see, I'm here this week," she finished. "Until Friday morning probably – we're not booked for the Mess, are we?"

"No, we're not," he agreed in a subdued tone.

Barbara looked closely at him. "Look, I'm sorry I upset you last Friday," she said. "It was thoughtless of me."

"No," he protested. "You were quite right – I shouldn't have let Josie in on our rehearsal…" He hesitated. "Anyway, she was very impressed," he said, brightening.

Barbara's heart sank. "Really?"

Theo nodded. "She especially liked my songs," he said a little shyly. "Thought they'd go well in a bigger setting…" Again he paused.

Barbara had the impression there was something he wasn't telling her. Had he accepted another gig? Gone ahead with the recording without consulting her? She quelled her angry thoughts. Better to take things calmly, she told herself.

"You know, Theo," she said, settling herself on the opposite bed. "I've been thinking…"

"So have I," Theo said sombrely.

"And have you come to any conclusions?" smiled Barbara.

"Well, actually the conclusions have rather come

to me."

Ah, she thought. So he has got something organized.

"What do you mean?" she asked.

Theo swung his legs down off the bed and planted his feet firmly on the floor, facing her.

"You see," he said, "I didn't think you'd be getting back at least for a few days – possibly all this week."

"Didn't Katie give you my message?"

"Oh yes – but by then it was too late…"

"Too late for what?" Barbara was really alarmed now.

"Well, to change things again." Theo looked down at his feet, then up at Barbara, his dark eyes filled with misery. "Wellworn Records want me to do some of my songs with a band backing."

"But Theo, that's great! Congratulations!" Barbara took his hand and squeezed it tightly. And all the time her mind was ticking over. If they made the recording with a band, she'd be committed – her decision to give up singing would never hold. Yet how could she refuse to do this for Theo when it was just the break he'd longed for? Inwardly she groaned, even as she smiled to show him how pleased she was.

"Well, that's the good news," said Theo, sitting back and removing his hand from her grasp. "The bad news is…" He paused.

"Go on!" Barbara commanded.

"They've got their own vocalist." He said it very rapidly, as if to get it over with.

"You mean – they don't want me?" Barbara didn't know whether to feel relieved or indignant.

Theo frowned earnestly. "It's not that they weren't impressed, Ba," he assured her, "it's just that they've got this band lined up and they have their own singer."

"And she's good?" Barbara asked him.

Theo nodded. "Very," he said quietly.

There was a thoughtful silence for a moment or two, then Barbara looked up.

"Good enough to take over the Wednesday gigs at Chuzzlewit's?" she asked.

Theo stared at her. "Well, as a matter of fact," he said, "I asked her to stand in for you this Wednesday. You see, I didn't think you'd be here and I couldn't afford to miss the chance—"

"Of course you couldn't," said Barbara, and she took both his hands this time. "Theo, it couldn't have worked out better. You know I've never been as keen as you are on a musical career; I was terrified I was holding you back. And since – well, since grandma died – I've worked things out. I want to stick with nursing, Theo – serious nursing. Degree, Master's – the lot."

"You mean you're giving up singing altogether?" Theo was unable to keep the relief out of his voice.

"You make it sound as if it was a good idea," she protested, laughing. "Was I so bad?"

"No — no you weren't — aren't," Theo said. "It was you got me kick-started. Remember Katie's revue last summer? I think that was the first time I realized I could make something of my talent. Working with you — with your voice — has been the best thing that's happened to me at St Ag's, Ba. I'm only sorry we won't be working together again."

"Oh yes we will," smiled Barbara. "I've got a booking for us on Thursday afternoon."

"You've what?" he asked, amazed.

And she explained about her promise to Evie Wilde.

"You will do it, won't you, Theo?" she pleaded. "Our last appearance together…"

Theo smiled. "Of course I will. Nice to end on what you might call an off-beat note."

Barbara laughed and for a moment they looked at each other fondly.

"And after that?" she asked softly. "You're giving up medicine?"

"I certainly am!" Theo grinned. "Once I've finished here I've done everything my parents wanted. I'm their eldest son, the doctor. My brother's going to be the lawyer." He grinned deprecatingly. "It was expected, you know. But I never promised I'd go into practice. When I finish here, I'm going to do it my way — in the music business."

"And good luck to you, Theo." Barbara reached over and hugged him. "One thing's sure – you're a better musician than doctor," she said. "Your pal out there told me to remind you you owe him tonight's duty."

"Oh hell!" Theo slapped his head.

"So you'd better come and get some food inside you." Barbara stood up. "I was going to the cafeteria anyway. We can celebrate the end of our beautiful partnership," she said. "And the start of your new life!"

The cafeteria was almost deserted at that twilight time between departed visitors and staff change-over. And for the first time for days Barbara felt really hungry.

"Go on, have what you like – it's all on me," said Theo expansively.

"Steady on! You haven't got your golden disc yet," Barbara teased him. But she helped herself to lasagne and a large coffee.

They settled themselves in "Kelham Korner" and Theo listened whilst Barbara told him about Grandma Robinson.

"She was all alone, Theo, that's what I can't get over. I mean what sort of a health service is it that lets an old lady die in an almost deserted ward, all on her own, while she waits for results of tests that might have saved her life?"

Theo sighed. "I'm so sorry, Ba," he said. "All I can say is I don't think it would happen here at St Ag's."

"It won't happen anywhere if I get my way," said Barbara fiercely. "Once I'm qualified I'm going to upgrade my accountancy qualifications, do my Master's in administration and damn well help to get this dying health service on its feet again!"

"And you can do it, too – I know you can," said Theo, warmly. He leaned across and touched her cheek. "Nothing like a bit of work to cure heart-ache," he said softly.

Barbara grasped his hand and held on to it for a moment.

"You sound just like my grandma," she told him and they laughed. They were still laughing when Barbara glanced over towards the door and saw Mel Craster sitting nursing a coffee. Their eyes met – hers alarmed, embarrassed; his puzzled, hurt.

"Damn!" she said aloud.

"What is it?" Theo asked, following her gaze. "Or should I ask who?"

"Oh – he's in charge of Geriatrics while Coulthard is away." Barbara contrived to sound casual.

"Oh – your boss, so to speak?" he teased.

"*You* might think in those terms," said Barbara crisply. "Nurses don't."

"Well, I don't know what you've done to him but he's looking across here like thunder," smiled Theo.

"I expect he thinks I should be sunk in gloom after this weekend," said Barbara, spearing a piece of broccoli viciously. "But that's the last thing Grandma Robinson would want."

Nevertheless, she was suddenly smitten with a pang of guilt, though whether it was caused by Mel Craster's puzzled glance or the memory of Grandma Robinson she wasn't quite sure. "I'd better get back to Kelham's anyway," she sighed. "Ring home and see how they're all getting on."

Theo stood up as she left. "Thanks, Barbara," he said, putting his hand out to her, "for everything."

Aware that Mel Craster could still be watching, she shook Theo's hand decorously. "Good luck, Theo – and don't forget our final gig, Thursday afternoon!"

"Positively your final appearance?" he teased.

Barbara hesitated. "Let's say possibly, shall we? 'Bye!"

She walked towards the exit knowing she'd have to face Mel Craster. Knowing too, how intimate that little scene with Theo must have looked to an outsider. Well, she owed Mel an explanation, she decided, after he'd been so kind. She braced herself and produced a brilliant smile.

But Mel Craster had gone.

Chapter 11

The week slid by at an alarming rate. Tense and anxious, Barbara couldn't decide what was bugging her most: Evie's concert, the ever-looming exams, or Grandma Robinson's funeral.

This last was eventually sorted. To her surprise, it was her father who rang with the news.

"Looking forward to seeing you again, Barbie-gal!" he said. "Been too long, you know."

"I know, but you can't take trips out to Jamaica on a student grant."

"Nor back to England on freelance journalism, gal, believe me!"

She heard his deep, rumbling laugh and suddenly felt like she used to when she was a little girl – miserable and upset about some triviality, until he'd appear in the doorway like the sunshine, exuding warmth and light and comfort.

Her eyes filled with tears. "Oh, Dad!" she said huskily. "I'm glad you're home." She sniffed and added, "How's Ma?"

"Oh, you know Selina – coping magnificently as she always does."

"And Grandma? Have they done the autopsy?"

"All over now," he reassured her. "Seems she'd been heading this way for some time. Transient schematic attacks – is that what they're called, Nurse Robinson?"

"Ischaemic," Barbara corrected him. "And I'm not a nurse – yet."

"You will be," he assured her. "And according to Selina, a very good one too, but then…"

"She would say that, wouldn't she?" Barbara rejoined, and they both laughed at the family joke: Selina Robinson was always fiercely supportive of her children.

"Rob tells me you're still singing," her dad went on pointedly.

"Not any more," she said firmly. "I'm going to concentrate on my medical career."

"But you will sing for Grandma, won't you?" He meant at her memorial.

"Of course I will. Positively my last public appearance," she said, echoing Theo's words.

"The funeral's at three on Friday – just family.

The memorial service in church Saturday morning will be a full house. You can choose the songs – Grandma's favourites, you know?"

"Yes, Dad, I know. I'll practise a few during the week."

"Good girl. Let me know the train times – I'll be there to meet you."

"Thanks, Dad. See you!"

"Love you!" he said, and put the phone down, leaving Barbara smiling tearfully down the mouth-piece.

She found a good opportunity to practise some of Grandma Robinson's favourite songs at rehearsals with Evie Wilde, who had hit on the great idea of mixing Jamaican folk songs with some numbers from English musicals.

"You see most popular songs deal with the same themes – lovers' fond meetings and sad farewells, toil and trouble, births and deaths…"

"Sounds just like home," Barbara smiled wanly.

Evie Wilde looked stricken.

"Oh, my dear!" she exclaimed. "How thoughtless of me – I am a fool! Here am I blabbering on about songs, and I hear you've lost your grandmother. I am so sorry. So very sorry!"

"Thank you, Miss Wilde," said Barbara. "That's really sweet of you."

Evie Wilde looked at her for a moment, then

extended her hand. "I wish you'd call me 'Evie'," she said simply.

Barbara smiled at this great honour. "Thank you – Evie," she said. "Tell you what, I'll sing you my Grandma's favourite – *Jamaican Farewell* – and you can do your *Goodbyee* – they'll all want to join in with those."

"Oh yes – that will make a wonderful climax to the programme." She scribbled hastily in her little notebook. "And of course it's very apt," she went on.

"Apt?"

"Yes. You're going back into the college, I'm going back home, so we shall be bidding farewells all round."

"So your housekeeper's come back?' asked Barbara, knowing full well she hadn't.

"Oh, her!" Evie made an extravagant gesture of dismissal. "I can manage without her."

"But you can't, Evie," said Barbara gently. "Even here you need someone to help you wash and dress, to bring your food to you, push your wheelchair... How could you possibly manage on your own at home?"

Evie sat bolt upright and stuck out her bottom lip like a sulky child.

"You're on their side," she accused Barbara. "You're going to let them keep me here like a prisoner." Her eyes filled with tears.

"Evie, they don't want to keep you here. This is a hospital, not an old people's home. You're not ill, you're just a bit frail – and you do need someone to look after you."

"You'll do," said Evie, brightening. "You're a good girl – we could sing together in the afternoons. I have my piano still…"

Barbara smiled and shook her head. "I can't do that," she said. "I have to go on with my course."

"But if you came with me I could train your voice – introduce you to theatre people – get you started…"

"Evie! You're not listening to me. I'm not going to be a professional singer – I'm going to be a nurse."

There was a pause. Evie fiddled with the tassel on her pen.

"I'll be all right," she muttered. "I'm expecting a phone call this very morning, you'll see!"

Barbara sighed; there really was no reasoning with the old lady.

"Look, I've got to get on the ward. Do you want me to push you over to see Harold Gough? He's really perked up on his new treatment."

But Evie shook her head and gazed past Barbara into the far distance.

On the ward Mark was checking charts and treatment regimes.

"Last week for you, Ba," he said. "Now, what can I offer you as a little treat? Oh, yes, I know – what about a few foot checks?" he smiled.

"Thank you," said Barbara ironically. "Where do I start?"

"Well, Mrs Hall's sitting out now. You know what to look for?"

"Of course. Didn't I have the best teacher in St Ag's to show me?" Barbara grinned. Mark had taught her the importance of checking the patients' feet for symptoms of oedema, varicose ulcerations, poor mobility, as well as the basic needs of chiropody. Collecting a sheaf of pink forms from the nursing station, she set off down the wards on her foot-check round.

The good news was that Mel Craster had a clinic day, so at least she didn't have to worry about meeting him suddenly in the corridor. The previous evening she'd decided she should ring him and explain that intimate little scene with Theo in the cafeteria. But she couldn't find his card and, of course, like most doctors, he was ex-directory. Barbara couldn't decide whether to feel frustrated or relieved!

And anyway, she told herself, as she knelt before Harold Gough and gently took off his slippers, why should she explain? Whatever her relationship with Theo was, it was nothing to do with Mel Craster.

"You're looking a lot better, Harold," she smiled up at the old man.

"Feeling it too," he agreed, nod-nod-nodding. "Done me the world of good coming in here," he said.

"And when are you going home?" she asked, gently pulling on his toes and rubbing them.

"I don't know exactly – Sister Tate's getting in touch with Marlborough House."

"Marlborough House," Barbara repeated thoughtfully. "Is that the residential home across the Brassington Road?"

"Yes, that's it. Lovely place it is too – you should see our gardens! We designed them ourselves last summer, you know..." He went on chatting as Barbara examined his feet, but she wasn't really listening until she caught the word "concerts".

"You mean you have concerts at Marlborough House?" she asked, easing his slippers back on.

"Oh yes – concerts, talks, slide shows, drawing, painting – we have a residents' committee who plan the whole programme." He hesitated. "I'm in charge of music," he said proudly. "I've got the best collection of tapes, you see."

Barbara got up and sat on the chair beside him.

"It sounds a wonderful place," she said. "Have you told Evie about it?"

He shook his head. "Well, she's not really the type, is she? Has her own flat and a housekeeper."

"It's a council flat and her housekeeper's gone and left her stranded here," Barbara explained.

141

"Oh, poor old Evie Wilde." Harold's bottom lip trembled – and it wasn't just a symptom of his illness now. "What is she going to do?"

"Well, they're trying to persuade her to go residential, but you know Evie – battle on to the end, she will."

"Not on her own, she won't," said Harold, quite firmly for once. "There's been a single room vacant for several weeks now at Marlborough House. I was going to tell her, but it's right at the back, and anyway I didn't think she'd be interested."

"Oh, I think she might well be," smiled Barbara. "Especially if you tell her about the musical afternoons…"

And suddenly it was Thursday and time for the Tinsdale Musical Afternoon. To Barbara's surprise and delight, Theo had managed to take the whole day off, so Evie had a wonderfully bossy morning rehearsing him and rearranging the whole programme so that Barbara, who was busy being a nurse, had no idea what she was singing when.

"Don't worry, darling!" Evie was in expansive mood, basking in the music – and the attentions of a young man. "We have it all under control, don't we, Theo?" She leaned towards Barbara, confidentially. "He's a brilliant young man, this; you'd never think he was only a doctor, would you?"

Barbara smiled. Some people might think a

doctor's status far higher than a musician's – not Evie.

"Oh, it's almost like the old days!" she sighed. "I've had some delightful accompanists in my time!"

I'll bet you have – probably for breakfast, thought Barbara.

"I wonder if I could fit in a dance…" mused Evie.

"You'll have Sister Tate after you if you so much as attempt to walk across the room," said Barbara firmly. "If you're a good girl we might just let you stand up to take your bow."

That was just what she did – with great aplomb. Evie had planned the programme like the trouper she was: sentimental ballads following cheeky Jamaican calypsos, with a rousing audience number every now and then – "just to make sure they're awake," she'd smiled. Inspired by her enthusiasm, Theo was soon improvising around music-hall songs with the right touch to cover Evie's weakening breath or shaky top-notes. After all this, he had little time to spare for working on Jamaican folk songs so Barbara opted to sing unaccompanied, save by the tappings and hummings of her audience, who picked up the calypso rhythms remarkably quickly.

Towards the end of the programme she taught them *Jamaican Farewell*, weaving in and around the

wheelchairs and zimmers, leading the doubtful
wobblers or wavering grunters in the chorus:

"And I'm sad to say, I'm on my way,
Won't be back for many a day…"

Over and over again, until they swayed and clapped
in time to the now-familiar theme.

Then Evie took over. With no attempt to teach
her audience anything, she merely stood – holding
on to the piano, head erect, voice ringing with her
beautiful head-tones:

"Goodbyeee!
Don't cryee!
There's a silver lining
In the skyee…"

And finally they stood together, leading staff and
residents in a two-part harmony based on both
songs. Amazingly enough it worked – in fact, it was
terrific! Led by an ecstatic, if wobbly, Harold, the
audience clapped and cheered as they took their
bow, with Barbara holding firmly on to Evie.

"Wow!" gasped Evie uncharacteristically, as she
fell back into her chair. "I knew we could do it!"

"And we must do it again some time," said
Barbara, winking across at Harold.

"Could you?" he said, picking up his cue. "It

144

would be delightful to hear you over at Marlborough House."

"Oh, Marlborough House – it's all you ever talk about," said Evie sharply. "According to you there's nowhere like it."

"No, there isn't," said Harold. "It's the perfect place to live. Only one thing missing."

"Oh, you admit there is something wrong with the place, then?" Evie said triumphantly. "What's that?"

"You don't live there," Harold said simply.

And, to Barbara's amusement, Evie had the grace to blush. She decided it would be tactful to leave them alone to discuss their future plans.

She went over to the piano. "Thanks so much for doing this for me, Theo – it's meant a great deal."

"My pleasure," he said with a deep bow. Then he sighed. "I've got to go now, white coat time again – only a few more weeks though!"

"Good luck, Theo! Keep me posted. Your fans from St Ag's will always come to one of your gigs, so long as you don't get too pricey!"

"For you, comps!" he grinned. " 'Bye, Barbara – and don't neglect that talent." He blew her a mocking kiss.

"What – nursing, you mean?" she asked innocently.

"No, I do not. Music's just as important as Medicine – remember that!"

"As if I'd ever forget," she said. " 'Bye, Theo –

good luck!" She stood for a moment and watched him rush off across the foyer, late again!

"White coat time," she smiled to herself, and turned back to help Mark tidy up the Day Room. But her path was blocked.

"Congratulations, Barbara!" Mel Craster said. He took her hand and shook it – several times. "A thoroughly therapeutic afternoon – well done!"

"Thank you, Dr Craster," she said primly, trying to extricate her hand from his and move away.

"Wait – Barbara!" He grasped her hand so tightly now that it almost hurt. "Look, I realize now that I misinterpreted your relationship with Theo Britner. Stupid of me!"

"Yes, it was." She looked at him levelly. "But it's partly my fault too. I wanted to ring and clear things up, but I'd lost your card."

"I'll give you another." He let her hand go and patted his pockets vaguely. "Only I don't seem to have one with me."

"Well, I don't need it now, do I?" she smiled. "I'm going home tomorrow anyway – for the funeral."

They stood in silence for a moment, surrounded by people milling all around, pushing tea-trolleys, wheelchairs, carrying tables.

"When are you leaving?" he asked at length.

"Tomorrow morning – eight o'clock train."

"May I drive you to the station?" he asked in his formal manner.

Barbara nodded. "Yes, please," she said. "But won't you be on duty?"

"I'll get back here in good time," he assured her. He stood for a moment, fiddling awkwardly with the pens clipped to his white coat pocket. "Well, until tomorrow then – about seven-thirty?"

"Seven-thirty," she agreed, looking up at him and smiling.

And he smiled back, deep and direct, into her eyes.

"So – it's off with the uniform, on with the jeans!" Katie Harding announced over coffee that evening. "It's a pity you'll miss our unwinding weekend, Ba."

"Katie!" Claire admonished her. "Show a bit of tact, please!"

"That's all right," smiled Barbara. "Oddly enough, I'm really looking forward to my weekend with the family."

"Unfinished business," said Jan wisely.

"Yes, that's just it," Barbara agreed. "Once I've said goodbye to Grandma Robinson I'll be ready to come back and face things here."

"Just in time for revision week," Claire observed.

The Kelhamites all groaned.

"And after that, exams," said Nick Bone.

"And the end of the first year," said Jan portentously.

"End of an era, it feels like," said Katie. "Remember that afternoon in the common room when we first arrived?"

"Do I?" laughed Nick. "I thought you were a right little bossy-boots madam!"

"And I thought you were the dishiest feller I'd ever met!" Katie mocked. "Remember how I swooned at your feet?"

"Only because you fell over Nikki's luggage." Nick laughed – and everyone joined in.

"We are all different now," Jan observed sagely. "It has been a year of changing."

There was a silence as each one of them tried to remember all the things that had happened in the past year: placements, exams, lectures, seminars, discos, dances, fallings-out and falling back in again, holidays at home, terms back at their second home – Kelham House.

"Well, here's to the second year together," said Katie, lifting her glass. Sister Thomas had given her blessing to their taking over the first-floor flats, and, to everyone's relief, both Nick and Nikki had opted to stay on so that the Kelham Six would be together for at least another year.

"Our second year together!" they chorused, clinking their glasses of Claire's father's second-best "fizz".

"And our exams," added Jan mischievously.

* * *

All the way to the station Barbara could hear Mel humming *Jamaican Farewell* softly – and tunefully – to himself.

"You like Folk?" she asked.

"Some of them," he grinned.

"Music, I mean."

He shrugged. "I like anything when you sing it," he said. "Are you really giving it all up?"

"Not yet," she said. "I'm singing tomorrow at Grandma's memorial."

"Oh – just hymns?"

"Not what you'd call hymns," she said. "Gospel, with a bit of Jamaican."

"I wish I could hear you."

There seemed to be no answer to that. They drove on in silence until he pulled up on the station forecourt.

He turned to her.

"Will you sing for me some time?" he asked.

"Well, I think I could do that without compromising my principles," Barbara smiled. "After all, it'll hardly count as a public performance will it?"

He shook his head.

"Private," he murmured. "Very private." He reached out and picked up her hand, examining it thoughtfully for a moment.

Barbara sighed. "Must get my train," she said. "Thanks for the lift."

He pressed a card into her hand, folded her

fingers over it and bent to kiss them. "Try not to lose it this time," he said. "Ring me when you know what time you're coming back. I'll be here."

"Yes," she said, looking at him seriously. "I know you will."

She leaned over and kissed him, lightly at first, as if in a friendly farewell. Then he caught her shoulders, pulled her to him and kissed her full on the lips – a more than friendly gesture.

"Till Sunday, then," she said shakily when he eventually released her.

Barbara settled into her seat and watched the station platform recede as the train pulled away. She felt Brassington, St Ag's, and even Kelham's fade, as if they were all part of another life. Now she was off to face her family: her father, whom she hadn't seen in three years; her beautiful, brave mother; her irritating, much-loved brothers – and Grandma Robinson's farewell party.

"Goodbye, Grandma Robinson," she murmured. "You were right, of course – nursing and singing don't mix. But I'll sing for you tomorrow – my final public appearance."

She lifted her hand up to flick one solitary tear from her cheek, suddenly aware she was still clutching Mel's card. Smiling, she tucked it under her watch strap and sat back, gazing dreamily out at the wasteland of old, dead industries as if drinking in the most beautiful view in Europe.

Then, shaking her head, clearing her thoughts, she reached into her bag and produced a nursing manual. But before opening it, she paused, her attention caught by the rhythm of the wheels, where she thought she could hear Grandma Robinson's throaty chuckle.

"No point wastin' three hours moonin' outa that window, Barbie-gal, when is work to be done!"

Smiling, Barbara opened up her textbook and began to read.

Follow six student nurses as they come to terms with
doctors, patients, study ... and each other.

NURSES

Bette Paul

All the thrills of a busy Emergency Room,
from the ever-popular Caroline B. Cooney.

EMERGENCY ROOM

**CITY HOSPITAL.
EMERGENCY ROOM. And
the evening has only just
begun...**

**6.00 p.m. Volunteers Diana
and Seth arrive – eager to
help save lives...**

**6.38 p.m. Emergency – gun
shot wound – victim of a
deadly drug battle...**

**6.55 p.m. Suspected cardiac
in Bed 8. Another routine
heart attack? Not for
Diana...**

**7.16 p.m. All systems go –
Alec, sixteen, clings to life by
a thread.**

**This is the Emergency Room.
Precious seconds are ticking
away, and Diana and Seth
hold the balance between life
and death...**